AUTHOR	CLASS
LIVINGS, Henry	F

TITLE	No
Flying eggs and	204537975.
things	**01485005**

FLYING EGGS
AND THINGS

FLYING EGGS AND THINGS

More Pennine Tales

Henry Livings

Methuen

*The illustrations in the text
are by Maria Livings.*

First published in Great Britain 1986
by Methuen London Ltd
11 New Fetter Lane, London EC4P 4EE
Copyright © Henry Livings 1984, 1986
Illustrations copyright © Maria Livings 1986
Printed in Great Britain

British Library Cataloguing in Publication Data

Livings, Henry
    Flying eggs and things: more Pennine tales.
    I. Title
    823'.914[F]   PR6062.19

    ISBN 0-413-40830-2

Contents

Acknowledgements

'Industrial Injury'
was first published in *The Guardian*.

'There's Money in Cards'
was first published in *Fiction Magazine*.

Several of the childhood stories
were first broadcast on BBC Radio 4's 'Morning Story'
under the title 'Flying Eggs and Things'.

FLYING EGGS
AND THINGS

WHAT SHAPE'S A DUCK?

'What shape's a duck?' she said.

A figure like a child's scrawl, all straight lines with a blob in the middle, large dark opaque eyes. Lillian Bentham confronted me in the Square, tremulous, determined. I wanted an ounce of tobacco from the Post Office; I sought about for a quick answer, and an escape.

'There's ducks on the river Lillian,' I said, 'you could go and look; I haven't a lot of time see.'

'Its meat's all dark,' she said. 'Who's going to eat it? Alex thought it was a chicken when he bought it in Ashton. What shape's a duck? is it all flat?'

'There's four or more people keeps ducks round here,' I said. 'Cowboy'll kill you one, pluck it and dress it for you while you're there; then you'll know it's a duck; and you'll have to excuse me. . .'

'I don't want a duck,' she said, 'I think I've got one already. And I faint when I see blood.'

I sometimes have the feeling that Lillian'll disintegrate, like an old umbrella, in the gusts of life's buffetings; angular, difficult to dispose of; I didn't want to be there when it happened. Also Sam's very sharp on half past twelve, and Wednesday afternoon's Post Office business only. You have to go to the next village for shop business. Tuesdays it is there, for Post Office business only. . . I could sense the cogs of my mind slipping.

'Lillian,' I said, 'I don't want this conversation;
I don't believe it; please could you stop it now?
Everybody knows what shape a duck is. Is this
Tuesday or Wednesday?'

She thought about it for a moment.

'I think it'd be Saturday, I'm not sure,' she
said.

'WHEN?'

'When Alex got this chicken. What shape's a
duck? You're not to shout at me. Alex shouted
at me. Over the duck.'

Nobody ever sees Alex out; he sits at home, in a
shadowed corner, his life a silent transfixed martyrdom to
Lillian's martyrdom, with occasional snarls of grief.

'I need some tobacco,' I said.

'Alex has given up,' said Lilian, 'except he's
started again; he was hallucinating.'

'Given up what?' I said.

'Smoking,' she said, 'did I say he'd started
again?'

'Yes,' I said.

'D'you want a roast duck? you like country
things; nobody'll eat it at our house; we were
expecting chicken you see.'

Sam didn't respond well when I asked him for an ounce
of ready-rubbed duck; maybe he thought I was being
satirical about their Karen.

'It's twelve thirty,' he said, 'you can see the
clock.'

'Not if you stand here it isn't,' I said, 'twelve
twenty-nine and a half it says.'

He unlocked, came out from behind the counter, slow,
his eye on me; he looked up.

'Twelve thirty,' he said.

'Sam, I shall be hallucinating, and you'll be the

14

direct cause,' I said.

'I've been on my feet since four o'clock this morning,' he said, 'with the papers, and then the post.'

'Oh yes, we've got Miss Charnock's *Morning Star*, I was going to bring it up with me, only I forgot.'

He served me my tobacco, violently.

'Shop business nine am tomorrow,' he said. As I left, I could hear him in the back, quarrelling with Pauline about Miss Charnock's *Morning Star*.

I circuited the Square, vigilant for Lillian, close to the walls, slight spot of pain centred on the left-hand side of my chest; froze by the open shop door of Arthur Lees, greengrocer. Lillian was helping him empty his deep-freeze of corpses. She was holding a twenty-five-pound polythene-wrapped parcel in her frail arms; breasted like a dowager duchess it was, thighs of a Nureyev.

'Now that's not a duck is it Arthur?' she was saying.

Arthur bent over the cabinet, flushed, hauling out yet more packages, trout stored for Gel Bradbury, Mr Pepper's venison in brown paper, chickens, chickens, chickens.

'It's not duck-shaped is it Arthur?' said Lillian.

I didn't catch anything Arthur said, I think he was weeping.

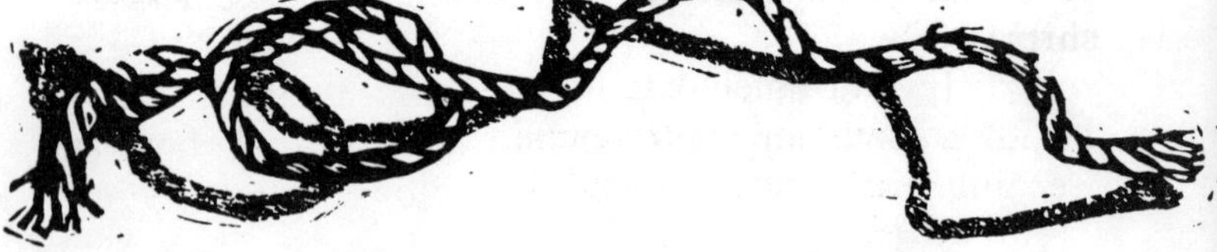

INDUSTRIAL INJURY

Harpo's bad backs are legendary. They're usually brought on by jobs that don't give space for his creative energy, or works time clocks that can't be manipulated to sort with his sleeping habits. Since he works with intelligent application when he is there, I've never seen the sense in requiring him to punch a time clock: the job gets done, you get the latest instalment on the current saga, so why isn't everybody happy? He was ten days taming the Dyeworks time clock: now it punches whatever time you care to call. But his back was agony until he'd got the clock docile.

He was coming to the taxi-service next door. I was getting the milk.

'Morning Des,' I said.

'Aaaah,' he said.

It was an unearthly castrato, like an ancient, mildly surprised hen.

'I'm extremely late for business, due to an unfortunate contretemps with a piece of string,' he said, 'aaaah, I shall have to have recourse to a hackney carriage.'

And he sat down on our front doorstep.

'It's no use, I shall be obliged to tender my resignation, regular hours are undermining my constitution.'

'How did a piece of string make you late for work and damage your constitution Desmond?'

'A disastrous concatenation of events,' he said,
'I also entirely forgot to take breakfast.'
'D'you want a cup of tea? I'll tell Harold you
want a car.'
'You'll have to bring it to me here.'

I went to brew. It was just after the Christmas holidays, lot of ice about. I didn't like to think of him on the doorstep. He'd not been right since the Children's Christmas Party. He'd volunteered to be Father Christmas, and Nipper Schofield, who was organizing it, had arranged for the Ledbury's donkey to be available, so that Harpo could arrive on a suitably biblical mount, laden with parcels. Unfortunately, as Nipper has a habit of saying, there'd been a bit of a hitch, lot of people had let him down over the Draw, very late in returning the stubs, could the Christmas Party be put off till February? Nipper was russet with moral indignation at being asked to resign from the Committee, and to explain the missing Draw money. A swift whip-round at the Shanter, the Bowls Club, and the Tinker and Budget put the Fund back in the black, but Harpo was left with the job of collecting the donkey. Nipper said he was deeply shocked at the attitude of the Committee, and was taking Angela to a first-class hotel in Blackpool over Christmas, 'away from it all': he didn't care to be pilloried, he said, by the modern equivalent of the Parisian mob, so we could stuff the donkey.

Harpo accepted the extra duty calmly.

'I have a certain affinity with animules,' he said,
'our cat converses with me daily.'

We waited in the Methodist Schoolroom, in a rising mutinous roar of children. The cakes and the jellies were long eaten, the prizes for 'Heads Bodies and Legs' distributed (the more pornographic submissions shoved privily under the door of the Hymn Book cupboard, please God somebody remembered to get rid of them afterwards), 'Statues' no longer capable of containing the children's frenzy. Father Christmas was coming, but when? Mr Bacon stuck his head round the inner door, unable to believe the volume of noise. He'd seen a figure, he bellowed in my ear, in a scarlet coat and white beard, by the canal lock, pulling on a rope tied to a small horse, and carrying a sack; was he anything to do with us? he seemed to be muddy. He'd told Bessie Medlar, and she'd said there was nothing in the Birth of Christ, she said, so far as she knew, that meant you had to get into a public house with the Co-op staff and make yourself poorly. He'd be better off giving them a decent wage. Bessie likes the Midnight Watch Service, and that's about all the Christmas she can take. Her two aunts from Cheshire are macabre.

The children had given over attacking each other, and were beginning to attack Committee members. I kept the smile going, but it stiffened: the game they'd invented, quite constructive in its way, seemed to need my shins as train-buffers once in a while. The look of hot sweaty malice on Polly Whitaker's bonny little face was a wonder: so much anger in so small a compass. Clingfilm said he'd go and get Harpo in the car, if somebody could give him an idea of where he was by now.

'It's the donkey and the presents more than anything,' I said, 'and I don't see you getting a donkey into your car.'
'You could hold the halter through the window,' he said, 'and it'll trot along beside us.'

I could see myself getting into something I couldn't finish; it felt like one of Harpo's obsessions, working at long distance. Kinetic transfer? I went outside to gulp some fresh air, and to ease my eardrums.

He was coming up the hill from the Square, the halter rope taut over his shoulder, the perspiration dripping from his face in a glittering curtain, the beard dangling vertical from his ears. The donkey seemed affable enough, giving an occasional shake of its head, which put Harpo off balance and cross-legged. It was probably animal intelligence, because as the man staggered sideways, the halter slackened, and the beast had a chance of a bite of roadside grass. The rough sack of parcels was tied to the saddle. I hurried to him.

'Had a modicum of inconvenience with this animule,' he said, 'it has its own notions.'
'Get on its back,' I said, 'the children are waiting.'
'I tried that, slid off during one of its gyrations, into those reeds by the Arches.'

His trousers clung round his calves, sodden, when he moved I could hear water slurping in his Wellingtons, there were bits of greenery and brown slime on the sack.

'I think the presents may be a trifle moist,' he said.

I heartily wished Nipper was there, as scapegoat; he's used to this sort of thing. I gripped the saddlegirth as the donkey skittered sideways, thumped it on the rump to get it off my foot. A window opened. I hadn't the leisure to look, but knew it was Mrs Gartside, who misses nothing:

'I shall report you to the RSPCA,' she called, calm and lofty, and closed the window again.

As I scuffled with the beast, I could see the headline: Santa Claus and Accomplice Fined for Maltreating Donkey. With ordinary luck, the *Advertiser* would misspell my name.

We made it to the schoolroom door, whence the din continued, a hornets' nest, stoking its own fury. Harpo mounted, slung the sack over his shoulder in the traditional style.

'Right,' he said, 'let her go.'

20

As I opened the door, the donkey seemed to sense the prospect of love within; ears up and questing, it moved sedately into that scrubbed, Lysol-scented room, among yellow and blue flimsy paper chains, sagging balloons. The donkey-star. The banshee yelling of the kids fell away, an audience of mouths, and then Polly, ever the demagogue, voiced the general awe in a low drawn-out vocalized sigh. Never mind that the tissue wrapping on the tawdry presents was pulp rags, never mind that Father Christmas stank ten men's height of canal water, sweat, and the Shanter's best keg. ('I thought I'd better call in and not pass,' he told me later, 'I owed Frederick five pound.' I know full well why he went in there, he wanted to be sure everyone had clear evidence of the facts on which he would be basing the next saga; the donkey had had a pint of dark mild, on the house.)

The children crowded round, entranced; and that spattered, scruffy, ill-proportioned animal turned into myth; hosannahs of childish murmurs, small hands reaching out to touch the bearer of Christmas, pink plastic water pistols, wind-up terrapins and tortoises for the bath, swap you Vanessa, seen for the tokens they were, and contentedly accepted, 'Father Christmas knows my name mum'. Harpo promised each and every one their heart's desire, and it was so; for half an hour, nothing was impossible. I had to take the donkey back to Bredbury's: Harpo was high on performance adrenalin, and anyway he'd ricked his back; after the limelight, the lime-boy goes home to cocoa.

The kettle boiled, and I took him out a mug.

'There'll be a car for you in a few minutes,' I said, 'what about the piece of string?'

'It was my method of getting up on time,' he said. 'I tied this piece of string to the hammer of the alarm clock, then I attached the other

end to a biscuit tin lid, which I placed on top of
the shade of the reading lamp on the dresser,
slightly tilted, with half a dozen of Nicky's
marbles in the tin lid . . .'

He was getting into the scene, tilting the shade of the lamp
with delicate rococo gestures, balancing the tin lid, plac-
ing the marbles as if counting out diamonds . . .

'. . . aaaah,' he said, 'I then placed the mop-
bucket strategically below, so that the smallest
agitation of the alarm clock's mechanism would
precipitate the marbles into the bucket.
The late-night film concluded at one-fifteen.
Maggie came to bed. Didn't put the light on,
for fear of disturbing my repose. Opened the
dresser drawer in search of a clean nightie, and
activated the whole contraption. Of course it
was totally effective in its purpose of waking me
up, sounded like violent musketry. Instead of
being impressed by my ingenuity, she was
enraged. Heaven knows what time I finally
slept, but at eight forty-five I started awake, full
of anguish and dread, pulled on my garments
and shoes in extreme haste, stepped upon one of
Nicky's marbles on the floor, executed a
perfectly splendid high-kick, and wrenched my
back again, most grievously. I shall have to give
up these regular hours you know, I've got
Industrial Lumbago.'

FLYING EGGS AND THINGS

My mate Bakey was always a flummin' liar. It got sometimes so there was no point asking him anything. Like what time's the next bus. Two hours he'd say. And you'd look round, and the flummin' bus'd be there, looming up. If you're daft enough you'll say I thought you said two hours till the next bus, and he looks at you as if you're daft, which you are, for asking, and he says 'I see no bus,' and he gets on it.

In my opinion he does it for practice. In case he gets captured by the enemy. Like I used to practice doing everything with my left hand, in case my right hand had to be amputated. I got in a right mess with a boiled egg. While my mother was putting the kettle on, with her back turned, I got a fork across the bottom of the egg cup, and pressed my right elbow on it to hold it steady; I reckoned it'd be best if I still had an elbow. Then I tapped gently all over the top of the egg with the spoon. When she came back to the table, I cracked on to be saving the egg, and chewed at the toast. She knew something was up, she kept giving me funny looks. 'Have you got your vest on?' she said. 'Yes,' I said. 'You've got a funny look on you,' she said, 'take your elbow off the table.' I had to wait till she went to fill the teapot.

I had the idea I'd be able to scrape off the broken bits of shell between my thumb and the spoon, but I had to keep the egg steady. I checked if the egg was firm in the egg cup. Left hand of course. Spoon ready. The man on the radio said it was eight twenty-seven. Kettle boiling. I thought she'd never get up. She burnt the kettle out once; said it was my fault. I kept watching the kettle, chewing at my toast. Bit of steam. 'Kettle's boiling mum!' I said. 'What's the matter with you?' she said, 'you think I'm not capable of telling if a kettle's boiling? you can see I'm reading the paper; you see to it if you're that bothered.' I tried to imagine myself carrying the teapot across left-handed, taking off the lid, lifting the kettle and filling the pot. The kettle lid falls off, it's loose, and you scald your knuckles if you don't hold it on with your other hand. Anyway what's the use? I'd never get to eat my egg left-handed; she'd be watching. The eight-thirty news headlines on the radio. I was going crackers. At last she got up.

The fork must have shifted itself, or else it had got jostled while I was worrying about the kettle. It wasn't my fault. I thumped my elbow onto the fork, quick; the egg cup flirted out sideways, and the egg flew through the air like a huge tiddlywink, so my mother dropped the teapot and the kettle trying to catch the egg. It was Star Wars in our kitchen.

I had to run to catch up with Bakey. I told him about the flying egg. 'That's nothing,' he said, 'I was flying this morning, all over the village, before anybody else was up.' 'You flummin' liar,' I said. 'I let the dog out for a pittle,' he said, 'and I was going to pick up the milk, when it suddenly came to me: if I fancied flying, I could, just by letting it happen.' 'Shut up Bakey,' I said; he made me feel strange. 'The dog was quite still,' he said, 'one paw up, its nose on a blade of grass, and I rose up over the crab-apple tree, then again, up. It's very quiet up there.'

I stopped, and I said, when I could think what to say, I said, 'You'd break your neck Bakey.' 'I thought you said I was a liar,' he said; 'The church weathercock's bigger'n me,' he said. 'I let myself hang straight by the side of it for a second, with my feet level with the ball at the bottom, and its head was exactly above me; I spread out my hand to measure its head, and without me even thinking it my body rose up and I lifted away in a great loop, and then another, as if it was a great big tremendous pendulum. I'm one metre thirty-two, and my hand-spread is fifteen centimetres.' 'If you don't just shut up, Bakey,' I said, 'I don't know what I'll do, but you'll be sorry.'

He shut up, and we walked on for a bit. 'What happened then?' I said. 'Our dog was a white dot in a little green square,' he said, 'with a splodge for the crab-apple tree. Still had its paw up. You know how Mr Gray always has a flower in his buttonhole when he's delivering the post?' he said. 'Oh yes?' 'Well he pinches it from Mrs Gartside's front garden.' 'Even Mrs Gartside knows that,' I said. 'All of a sudden I was back at our house again,' said Bakey, 'the dog finished its sniffing and put its paw down.' 'Dead boring,' I said.

We were late for Assembly of course, we always were.

First lesson was trigonometry. Old Clarky had a new toy to play with, looked like a little telescope on three big wooden legs. 'THIS, CHILDREN, IS A THEODOLITE,' he says, 'A VERY EXPENSIVE PIECE OF EQUIPMENT, DON'T ANY OF YOU DARE TOUCH SETTLE DOWN SETTLE DOWN! BY MEANS OF THIS, SURVEYORS CAN MEASURE AND MAP OUT LAND, GIVING DISTANCES AND HEIGHTS.' I've never had much luck with trigonometry since old Clarky explained how the sum on the hypotenuse is something to do with the sum of the other two sides by banging my head on the blackboard. 'THE HEIGHT OF THE WEATHERCOCK ON THE CHURCH CAN EASILY BE CALCULATED,' he was saying. . . I sat up. . . 'BY LOOKING THROUGH THE LENS, NOTING THE ANGLE ON THE

27

SCALE HERE, AND THEN LOOKING AT THE BOTTOM. WE KNOW THE WEATHERCOCK IS UPRIGHT, AND WE CAN MEASURE HOW FAR WE ARE FROM THE CHURCH.' He drew it on the blackboard.

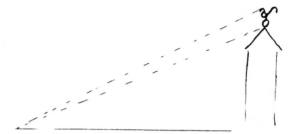

'SO THE DIFFERENCE BETWEEN THE TWO TRIANGLES IS THE HEIGHT OF THE WEATHERCOCK!' 'One metre forty-seven,' said Bakey.

The chalk broke in Clarky's hand. The room went quiet. He walked over to us where we sat. 'Who said that?' he said. 'Him,' said Bakey. Old Clarky gripped me by the jersey, and stared at me, close. I could see sweat start to trickle out among his tatty old ginger hair. Then he went back to the front and tried to carry on with the lesson. But he was watching me and Bakey all the time, so he didn't make a lot of sense to any of us.

How the flummin' heck did Bakey know a thing like that?

WHAT ARE NEIGHBOURS FOR?

'I've got something at home that'd interest you.' The voice
of Ken Major. I hoped it wasn't for me. A grizzled man,
complexion dark ivory, hair clipped to bristles, bony
frame; he squares up to tell you something as if you were a
periscope. Bessie Medlar he'd got this time; in the Co-op;
he came upon her from behind the sugar shelf, Nosferatu
in a flat cap:
> 'I've got something at home your Jimmy'll like,
> I heard he was asking.'
I slipped past, distributing a shifty nod, and beat them to
the checkout, but the voice sawed its way to me through
the clatter of trollies:
> 'Ram's horn, beauty it is, massive. He'll be in
> raptures, your Jimmy. I've seen some of the
> carving he does. I've done it over with surgical
> spirit, against the flies.'
The constant trucking and trading of a village is no
worse than whose turn is it to invite whom in a lonely city,
but it's no better either.
> 'You like old books,' a neighbour told me one
> time, 'I've come across a load of old books at
> me dad's: he's no idea of their value; I'll bring
> them down and you can have a look at them; be
> worth a lot of money to the right person, say a
> collector.'
Six weeks later I'd forgotten the sinking feeling, nearly;
he was there at the back door, with a large cardboard

31

case, sodden in unexpected rain. I got him into the kitchen. Half a hundredweight of *Readers' Digest*s, starting 1938.

> 'Prewar, those, I was reading one or two of 'um, fascinating; it's got about Mussolini, I can't just remember what, but you'll soon come across it.
> I don't want money for 'um, just so long as they're appreciated.'

Do you detect the request for a hillside rabbit? preferably this weekend, when Kevin will be visiting home? Well, it's there.

I suppose it's primitive, a desire to be of consequence to your fellows, the fine adjustments of status and mutual help . . . if you're doing well, do you take a bottle of good wine and risk being thought to crow good fortune, or a plonk like everyone else and risk being called a tightwad? . . . And suppose you take wine where no wine is required? oh dear. The man with much wards off envy with generosity; the man with little still shares, and his neighbours accept, sooner than be thought proud. Mind, some of it is fairly ruthless: Tippy Tumbler said he'd got me a tobacco pouch, I could have it. I didn't want a tobacco pouch, I prefer plastic cashbags from the bank, then I don't mind too much if I lose them. Still I had to have it, a gift from Tippy Tumbler: an orange rubber pouch, impregnated for ever with camphor from some dank wardrobe. I can't use this; everybody'll think I've got a permanent head cold. Good pouch that, he said, genuine rubber.

> 'I've given him a tobacco pouch,' he announced to the Tap Room of the Shanter, 'it won't cost him nothing; all I want is just a pint or two.'

Oh yes, the ram's horn.

> 'Funny you should mention a ram's horn,' said Bessie, 'my Jimmy was thinking he'd a fancy to

get hold of one if he could; he does lovely hand-carving, winter evenings, when he can't get out in the garden.'

'That's just what I said,' said Ken.

Bessie was getting as shifty as me; you don't really listen to what Ken says, you just hear him talking.

'Yes I know,' she said, 'shall I give you some money? I don't want you to mention it to him if you don't mind, it can be a birthday present; be something different.'

Ken said, mysteriously, that he'd a bit on at the moment, but he'd be sure to let her have it in good time, and she wasn't to insult him with money, he'd always had a lot of time for her Jimmy. . . In fact he was still saying it as I slunk out of the shop, and it takes a good ten minutes to buy so much as a box of matches here; the counter staff tend to stack shelves or catch up on the Births Deaths and Marriages until there's a decent queue to go at. The subject of the ram's horn swirled briefly and then sank in the drone of Ken's voice:

'I'll settle for a lettuce or two some time. . .'

A sunny Sunday morning, on my way for the paper, my mind mostly enjoying that luxurious easing and stretching in your eyes as they adjust to new spring sunlight, when suddenly I was scalded by the sight of Ken, with his sister Elsie. It came to me that I hadn't seen her about, probably in years. Sometimes I took my walk past the house; she was a pale weak hand at the curtain, days upon days. You get used to the idea that so-and-so's not well; it's a violent shock when you see full the alterations of disease. Elsie Major's spine was so curved that her chin levelled with her shanks; her walk was crabbed and shuffling, obstinate; her complexion blue-white. Ken escorted her along the broken flagstones with tender reverence.

His voice contained the calm murmur of wood pigeons:

33

> 'Now see who's here Elsie, I bet it's months
> since you saw him.'

Her face, the features blurred by suffering, tilted so that
she could see me; a few random, meaningless syllables
bubbled out of her, cheerful; she crept painfully on
towards the paper shop.

> 'I made her come out,' he said, 'she'd stop in
> for ever and then come out in a box. You'll
> never get yourself right Elsie love, just sat in
> the house.'

How many years of constant loving care, unremitting
need? The big sister who bashed the lads who bullied little
Ken in the schoolyard. He's just past retiring, she's
around seventy; fifty years since their mother and father
died? This dull man, with nothing to offer, nothing of
consequence to say, no experience worth the repeating,
looks back and forward on decades of cherishing, for no
possible reward, and in return for no one's good opinion.
He'll say it of himself: 'Nothing ever really happened to
me, I've been lucky.' It was the radiant pride he took in her
that stopped me, you could see it from behind: his arm
curved in air above and round her shoulders, as if he held
an invisible net: his stricken Lazarus walked. I felt hum-
bled, stupid.

Bessie caught me by her gate, her lips blue with angina:
> 'Have you seen anything of Ken Major?'

I hadn't. He hadn't been in the Shanter for a week; the
word was Elsie wasn't so clever. Jimmy came into view
round the corner of the house, trundling a wheelbarrow
heaped high with rich, dark, midge-laden compost.

> 'He's promised me a . . . .'

said Bessie, then fixed me with eyes widened in complicity
and warning: two cabinet leaks in the presence of MI5.

Trouble for me, and for her husband, was that only Bessie knew what the leak might be about. Not only that, but the secret, whatever it might be, filled my mind exclusively, rendering me unfit for light conversation. Seeing me rooted, neither leaving nor passing nor chatting, Jimmy stopped, and set down the barrow. The first midge hit my eyelid almost simultaneously. I looked at Jimmy from under a thickening eyelid, my nose watering, a squadron of tickles in my scalp.

'Afternoon,' he said.

'Yes,' I said.

He didn't seem to notice that my reply didn't fit, more likely he was wondering why I was winking at him.

'I agree,' he said, 'but we could do with some rain.'

I have thickish eyebrows, the midges were moving in; compost for the main course, me for the gastronomes with fading appetites who like to toy with something tasty after the meal.

'Anyway,' said Bessie, 'if you'll just wait here, I'll get it for you.'

'What is it he wants?' said Jimmy.

'Shall you be wanting a brew before long?' she said.

'How d'you mean?' he said, 'you've only just this minute brought me a mug out the back.'

'Oh,' she said.

'And what's he waiting for?' he said.

'Good heavens,' she said, 'what kind of a man are you Jimmy Medlar? You mean a body can't wait in the street now?'

Jimmy looked hard at his compost, brows knitted. He hoisted the handles of the barrow again, tipped the contents between Bessie and me, withdrew, turned and departed without a backward look. Bessie didn't seem to

be troubled by midges. I wondered if a short sharp scream
would be socially acceptable.

'He's promised me a ram's horn,' she said.

My reply came out a sort of mangled falsetto:

'Who has?'

'Ken Major has. Got something in your throat
have you?'

'Midges mostly,' I said.

She didn't pause over it.

'The thing is,' she said, 'I haven't got anything
else for his birthday.'

'Jimmy,' I said, concentrating through an
invisible cloud of small fiery needles.

'Well who else? I don't think you're paying
attention.'

'Now that I've found out what I'm paying
attention to, I will do,' I said, grinding at my
scalp with a knuckle; when is a scratch *enough*?

'I can't get him any more whiskey,' she said,
'there's a sideboard full; and he hasn't smoked
his Christmas cigars yet; I thought it'd be
something different.'

'The ram's horn,' I said.

'Yes, and I'll swear one of the girls has said
something, he's been sharpening his jackknife. I
can't go round to Ken's now and say what about
this ram's horn: supposing he's forgotten all
about it? He said he'd bring it round, you were
there. Why do people say one thing and do
another? they don't know what they're doing to
folk.'

'I'm getting an idea,' I said.

Bessie's chomping anxieties made me anxious; I didn't
fancy the responsibilities she was chewing on for me.

'You know where he lives,' I said.

'Oh yes? and what do I tell Jimmy? I just
nipped round for a cup of sugar? a quarter of a
mile for a cup of sugar? anyway, it was
supposed to be a favour, how can you ask after
a favour?'

She gnawed at her bottom lip like a schoolgirl, pale eyes on
me, beseeching.

'I got him a card with a merino ram on it; he'll
think I'm losing my grip. Have you got a stye
coming on that eye?'

I routed myself past Ken's house; isolated, it looks as if
the plan was for it to be part of a terrace, too narrow to be
on its own. Maybe the builder had run out of money, or
maybe that was the only way he knew how to build.
Anyway, it looks odd, neighbourless, the grey lace across
the bottom half of the windows making it baleful, the
neglected paintwork sombre: the house needs addition to
make sense. I walked slowly, the corner of my sight alert
for movement within the house. No sign of Elsie. He slid
out, sideways, stern.

'Have you a minute?'

I waited.

'Only I promised Bessie Medlar something.
You'll be passing the house I dare say. Jimmy
hasn't to see what it is, it's to be a surprise.'

I kept my mouth shut; the untranslated network of
tomtoms spoke: I felt hooked-in to the Universe; I
remembered speckled trout, cold and slippery, an hour
out of the water, shoved at my feet in a plastic carrier bag,
a slow wink screwing up my mate's face like a door-
knocker; brown eggs with hen muck and straw stuck to
them, on the doorstep at first light, no sign of who they
were from, but I knew, I knew; the background music to
my brief reveries was Elgar, arranged for brass band,
played by Brighouse and Rastrick, in sepia.

'You can glance at it if you want,' said Ken.

The horn was wrapped in a sheet of the free newspaper; I peered down at it in the fading light, the bony fingers of an unformulated despair fumbling at my heart; there was something not quite right. The size.

> 'I wanted to get it decent,' he said, 'I've always had a lot of time for Jimmy; it won't cost Bessie a penny. What are neighbours for if you can't call on 'um?'

It was about the size of a ladies' umbrella handle, pale yellow, the pokerwork dots and whorls: a dead banana?

> 'I had a bit of trouble with bending it, getting the twists out; my uncle Norton used to do it as a hobby, plus I've got a book; it kept on getting burnt by the gas jet, and I kept on having to carve a bit more off. In the end I thought I know what, I'll decorate it with a red-hot poker, then you won't notice the imperfections. I've done a bit of pokerwork too, God Bless Our Happy Home, that sort of thing.'

His face, dark, hypnotic, intent, swam in and out of my attention: I was imagining conversation with Bessie; when would such a thing take place? Could I stand it tonight? Would I sleep if I didn't get it over?

> 'It was quite big when I got it,' he was saying; he looked as if he were listening to his own voice, in case nobody else did, and the sense of his words would be lost for ever. 'I thought maybe a shepherd's crook, but owing to unforeseen circumstances it's more of a decorative whatsit now isn't it? they could hang it on a wall. Anyway I've saved Jimmy a job.'

He stalked back to the house, paused to look out from the doorway, his eyes glittering in the dark lobby. I turned and went, hearing the thick old door thrust home and bolted. I stopped and looked at the object in my hand, wreathed in blotchy tattered newsprint; the adverts for second-hand cooking stoves, and snatched-back furniture had more dignity; I conjured an image of the rough noble sweep of animal power that had been crudely singed and scraped away, to make this thing, this congealed worm. Ken's voice climbed down out of the evening, monotone:

> 'Oh dearie me, look at the state, soaked again. Just feel at them sheets, go on, feel at 'um, or have you lost all feeling by now? senseless are you? Come on, let's be having 'um. You bloody old bag of bones, it'll be nappies for you from now on; I'm having you in Monkwood House, and think yourself lucky it's not the bottom block at the General Hospital, where they have all the other dafties; I'll get administration of your affairs, I will, you'll get cups of tea when *they* want, not when you want, and you'll pee to orders.'

Her loose, animal wail of grief pulled the dusk to pieces; I walked on, but his voice was inescapable:

> 'Now then, no crying, oh dearie me; no tears I beg of you; you know I'm only joking; you'll always have me, I'm your helpmeet Elsie.'

And then, through his crooning assurances, Elsie, momentarily clear, a bell-like descant:

> 'About as much use as a one-legged man in an arse-kicking contest.'

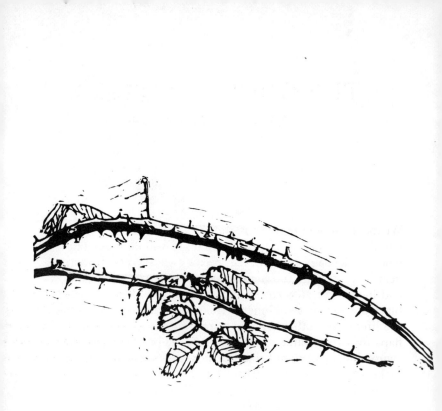

THE GHOST OF THE
MAD MONK

We'd been mucking about in the old Dyeworks for about a trillion years before Bakey decided it was haunted. The whole place was mysterious, and silent. Any noise you heard, it was you. You could lie on the bank of the dam and look down into the still clear water and see leeches, black and shiny, like slugs with no horns, waiting to suck the lifeblood of the unwary; water snails with triangular flaps for eyes; water scorpions that divided their tails to swim about and then brought the two halves together to make a tube to stick up to the top and breathe, and with nippers as big as the rest of their bodies.

There were stone archways onto the yard of the works, and underneath there were huge greeny glass jars, with their necks sticking out of wicker wrappers; huge, you couldn't lift one. And upstairs in the dyehouse, there was a big rusty iron hook swinging from a chain to an old girder over an oblong hole in the floor. You could swing across. Bakey swung across, and then I swung across, and all the rust got in your eyes and in your hair, and you could see the cobbles down below careering past under you. If you looked. You took a run, and a bit of a jump to reach the hook, and the old chain screeched along the girder a bit, and you were off the other side. Then you did it back again, screech screech. Once, I didn't swing hard enough to reach the other side, and I was wriggling like a worm to get back. I didn't like to think about the cobbles down there under my dangling feet; I squeezed my eyes up tight closed; the bits of rust were making them water.

'Give us a push Bakey,' I said.

'I can't reach you,' he said.

'I'll get you back for this,' I said, 'get a plank or something and give us a push, my arms are killing me, give us a push with a plank!'

Once, we found a raft in the Dyeworks yard, and we hauled it to the dam, and slid it down to the water over the reeds; well, it was a great big old door, all rotten; soon as it got out from the reeds, and we got onto it, it tilted, you could tell it wasn't going to be any good; about six feet from the shore, it went down; some raft, said Bakey.

'It's all right for you,' I said, 'I can't swim,' I said. He was whistling. 'D'you hear me?' I said, 'this raft's sinking, I'm going to drown, you'll have to life-save me; you said you've got your certificate, now's your chance.'

He took his clothes off, calm as anything, and chucked 'em onto the banking where his shoes and socks were. I thought I won't tell anyone, but he'll be the silent hero when it gets out; there'll be nothing from my mother about wet socks when she finds out how Bakey saved me from death by drowning. Then he lowered himself into the water, and did breaststroke to the side.

'I can't swim!' I said.

'Now's your time to learn,' he said.

'I'll get soaking wet, my mum'll play pop!' I said.

'Yes,' he said. He was rubbing himself dry on his jersey and socks and getting dressed. 'It must be nearly teatime,' he said, 'I'm getting hungry. See you.'

I took my clothes off as fast as I could, and threw them to the bank; I thought I'll lie in the water, like in the school

42

charts, so't he could hold my head up. I only hoped he wouldn't have to give me the kiss of life, he wouldn't miss a chance to pinch my nose, him. And then when I looked there was this lady, picking blackberries. I crouched down to cover myself. She was smirking away, I could tell, pretending not to look, getting blackberries. I didn't think there was anything funny going on. I hissed at Bakey:

'Life-save me you flummin' ape.'

'I've got to be going,' he said, 'I haven't got time. See you. My dad taught me to swim,' he said, 'he just chucked me in at the Baths, and I had to get out, it was freezing.'

I bet his dad did too; big mucky feller who never speaks. Only time he gets washed is when he's at the Baths I bet. Chuck anyone in he would. This lady stood up.

'What's that young man doing?' she said.

'He's sunbathing I think,' said Bakey.

'Don't you cheek me,' she said.

'Sorry miss,' he said.

'And I'm not a miss either,' she said.

I was crouched there, freezing.

'If you're planning on swimming,' she calls out to me, 'I suggest you use the Swimming Baths like a sensible person; it's no more than eighteen inches deep anywhere in that dam.'

Then she went back to her blackberry picking. It was hours. Bakey went home for his tea. Me on the raft, nude, six foot from my clothes. She said goodnight when she went, and perhaps I'd learnt not to be cheeky by now. I paddled to the bank and got dressed. Hanging on to that hook it came to me I never got him back for that either.

'That's where they hung the Mad Monk,' said Bakey; 'he hung there for days, until his arms stretched to twice their length, and the muscles of his shoulders wasted away, and he crashed to

his death on the stones beneath. Now his
tormented spirit haunts the Dyeworks on
Thursdays, moaning and gasping and doing
good works.'

His mother lets him stay up for ever, watching horror movies.

'What day is it?' I said.

'Thursday,' he said.

It was me that was doing the gasping and groaning, never mind the Mad Monk. I was sweating cobs and hanging on to the big hook, and my jacket all up round my ears, wriggling and shooting out a foot to get a grip on the other side, and all I could hear was Bakey, whistling. In the end I had to let my arms stretch out, my shoulders felt as if they were burning. I wondered if my arms would end up exceptionally long after this, and would it be any good for bowling. I'd have 'em folded up, when I wasn't bowling. My feet banged on wood. I opened my eyes and looked down. The trap door was closed. I stood on it, and let go the hook.

'Who closed the trap door?' I said; I was
fuming.

'The Ghost of the Mad Monk,' said Bakey.

THERE'S MONEY IN
CARDS

Dog's Doogle Eye is fascinated when he happens on the
Floating Bridge Game. It's not the cards, it's the money:
he'd quite like some of it. I don't play, so I don't know how
come a hundred pounds can change hands after a rubber
of bridge, but I've seen it happen. This is one of the
reasons it's a floating game: landlords get nervous.

The players vary; sometimes they let in the odd estate
agent, or a solicitor, but no matter how the personnel
changes, they all have a look of the winners of the St
Valentine's Day Massacre, crouched marble-faced over
their cards, huge pale fists on the table as if to show they're
not armed. On other evenings, they'll drink pints; if it's a
Bridge Night, a half of mild might be ordered in forty
minutes. Fred, the landlord of the Shanter, would sit
catatonic on a little three-legged stool behind the bar,
watching his electricity meter; Betty had to serve them,
and even then she had time to hoover all round upstairs
and dig the flowerbeds.

Once a night or so, the mortuary stillness is broken by
an unexplained eruption of shouting, tables over, 'That
was a no-trump bid you pitiful clown!', or some such; so
that strangers who a moment before were murmuring
respectfully to each other about nice quiet pubs will leave
half-finished drinks and sidle for the door with crab-like
speed. By the time the place is cleared of expensively
dressed casual trade, the card players are once more
hunched, silent and brutish, over the game. In the end

Fred, same as every other landlord whose premises the Floating Bridge Game used, asked them to move on.

Two pm, Thursday, the dead hour in the Tinker and Budget. Martin, the landlord, pop-eyed and hollow-cheeked, a grey slow-moving lizard, has just got up, and is bolstering his nerve with Complan and brandy. Dog's Doogle Eye stands like a lurcher at a rabbit hole: he's scented the Floating Bridge Game. Martin, forewarned, has locked off the side rooms, and put a sign saying 'DECORATION IN PREGROSS' on the wall, under the group photograph of the 1959 Mystery Trip. Jack Ledbury, small farmer and large demolition contractor, sits at the only table left available, seventy years old, with the folded neck, slabbed muscles, the sleepy grandeur of a Charolais bull, cracking his knuckles in the silence; next to him, property and small businesses (evictions a speciality), Arnold Brickman, rimless glasses, rimless eyes, stares before him like a cold-hearted buddha; and Colin Slattery, scrap, wrists as thick as another man's leg, hands like monkey wrenches curved either side of a new deck of cards, vibrating gently in neutral. They're waiting for a fourth.

Colin gets up, strides across to the gents, passing so close behind Doogle leaning on the bar that he involuntarily straightens himself out of the slipstream. Tap-tap go big fingers on the table top, tap.. tap goes Martin's glass at the brandy optic. Doogle's scratchy gabble penetrates the dusty air:

> 'I've got a good horse for the three o'clock; been given it by a feller.'

'Don't make trouble Stuart,' said the landlord.

His record is sixteen losers in one day's racing. The bets are so complicated, with doubles, trebles, Yankees, accumulators and Round Robins, there's a strong chance if they all come up, somehow Doogle will still lose. We once

tried to get the bookie to quote odds against him finding
one winner in a day's racing; the bookie said it would be
against his professional code and anyway he was going
away for a bit.

'Have I to put the jukebox on, for some music?
Anybody want the jukebox?'
Doogle talks, as often as not, for the same reason little boys
shout into empty barrels. Nobody else could love the noise
he makes but Doogle. Colin returned to his seat, swivelled
and sat in one movement, purposeful:

'Is that yours on the floor?' he said.

A fiver lay at Doogle's feet; he stiffened, bent swiftly,
stopped himself and then straightened, agonizing between
light-triggered covetousness and apprehension: if Colin
was having him on, he wasn't going to get the fiver; if the
fiver was Colin's, he still wasn't going to get the fiver
unless Colin said he was going to get the fiver. He couldn't
remember the last time anyone had prised a fiver off Colin
against his will, but he was fairly certain there must have
been a lot of blood. Good grief: supposing it was his own
fiver? Colin's eyes slant slightly, and he has light bristly
eyelashes; Doogle searched the face for mercy, and found
none.

'You just went by, could be yours.'
The landlord craned his frail frame over the bar to look
down, swivelling his head about to examine the
customers:

'That's a fiver.'
Doogle seemed to have a vision of Martin's bony claws
coming down on his fiver; he tensed up and began to
babble:

'Now just a minute, I changed a tenner in the
Co-op, anybody'll tell you that that was there,
Mrs Brierly, yes, she was there, that'll be the
way to tell; I paid Martin for one drink, you all

49

remember that, and if you don't accept it,
Martin'll have his till roll, so I should have
eight pounds in my pocket, plus shrapnel. I
distinctly remember Bacon giving me a fiver,
because it was an unusually clean one for a
Thursday. Thank you for pointing it out
Colin.'

You could nod off while Doogle is explaining ordinary
unremarkable events; he was palming the money from his
pockets hand to hand like an amateur conjuror, bungling
and feverish, one eye on the fiver. The other customers
watched, blank-faced, as he wove himself into an elaborate
knot, tucking in the ends, waiting for tacit permission to
pick up the note, which had not been denied.

'Yes, definitely, I'd say it was mine, must be.'

Jaunty, he bent to pick it up. It gave a couple of little
jumps along the floor. Doogle grabbed again, and was on
his knees before he'd worked it out that the fiver was
mobile. The note rose in the air as he grabbed a third time,
and sailed gracefully to the table as Arnold hauled in the
fine black elastic to which it was attached. When a hammer-thrower has loosed the hammer in athletics, he's
liable to hop a bit, I daresay you'll have noticed; well,
Doogle as he rose after the fiver, and lost it, hopped a
bit.

'That's very good that,' said Colin, 'could you
do it again?'

It wasn't all that good a jest when it came to hey-lads-hey; on the whole, played by the wealthy on the poor, it
was cruel. Doogle, however, looked on it as Next Stop the
Palladium, related it sniggering to every newcomer. .

'. . I had a good one done on me just now,
you'd a laughed your sides sore if you'd seen it
. . .'

. . . until the room was dotted with groups of people,

50

elbow to elbow to avoid his conversation. Even Jack Ledbury, normally as sensitive as a Newhey brick, seemed to suffer a fleeting remorse.

'Shut up you moonfaced prawn,' he said.

'You're right, you're right,' said Doogle, 'right, yes, I'll get this bet on. Eight to one winner, in the bag, past the post.'

The fourth had arrived; the players were brooding on their hands. Doogle hovered, wittering.

'This feller had two hundred off a stable boy to put on for somebody else, so you can tell its prospects. It had to go on off-course, so as not to raise suspicions.'

'By God that will shake Ladbrokes, two ton on the nose at eight to one,' said Arnold, without looking up; 'what's the horse?'

'Yes, you're right, I agree with you,' said Doogle, jigging at the door. 'Right, I'll be off now and get it on.'

Arnold looked up, without love.

'What's the horse?'

'Ah, now, that's something I can't tell you. I promised, right?'

Arnold slammed down his cards:

'Martin, pass us the newspaper; let's be seeing this eight-to-one wonder; three o'clock did you say?'

'Ah, now, it's not necessarily eight to one in that paper. And it could have altered at the bookies' by now. Might even be ten to one, or even sixty-six to one by now.'

Arnold threw the paper back over the bar, and tried to concentrate on the cards in his hand, but the other players were staring at Dog's Doogle Eye. And it's true the performance was fairly mesmeric; he seemed to be in the

51

grip of a furious storm of psychic energy, jigging and twitching.

'Right, yes, it's anonymous this horse. Till three o'clock. In case there's too much goes on and it ruins the odds. Stable boy's tip. Right.'

A muscle was ticking in Arnold's cheek; he looked up from his cards, controlled a spasm, spoke offhand.

'Put a score on for me.'

'Right Arnold. Oh, no, I'm not sure if I can do that, ethically, sorry Arnold, for all you're a pal of mine. Right. Tell you what, I'll tell just you, in strictest confidence, if you promise not to divulge it; then you can decide for yourself whether to back it or not.'

You could almost hear the clock clunk up to two forty-six. Arnold thrust a twenty at him.

'Bloody put it on, and I want to see the slip, or you'll be eating your tea through your arsehole.'

Martin came out of coma briefly.

'Take it Stuart, I'm having no fighting.'

Notes were selected from wallets, money belts, the five-furlong pocket, fivers, tenners, twenty-spots; Arnold gathered them up at speed, fanned them to reckon the amount, handed them to Doogle. Cowboy's intervention was a twig in a torrent:

'I'm going down to the bookies myself; have I to put it on for you?'

The door was just falling to behind Dog's Doogle Eye.

It was a poor game of bridge, no fighting and bawling. Doogle was back in time for a last legal pint. The telly was turned up for the three o'clock race, and they were off. Doogle's horse, now unveiled as Hotbed, led from the start. The money was on, he said, at thirteen to two. Expressions didn't alter round the table, but there was a sort of inaudible click as four finely tuned financial brains worked out the win, before their eyes went back to the screen. Favourite Paddyspad trailing in third place, Hotbed comfortably stretching his lead to two and a half lengths. . lovely day here at Newbury and Paddyspad has a lot to make up if he's to maintain his form this season and it's Hotbed now Welcome moving up and it's Hotbed then Welcome and Paddyspad vying for second place, Damhead then Birdie and it's Hotbed, Hotbed. .

The eyes of the room fixed on the little screen above the bar, feet drawing unconsciously nearer, chins tilted up in the silver light. . and it's still Hotbed from Welcome *and* Paddyspad fighting it out for second place Paddyspad moving up into second place and he's closing the gap Paddyspad putting on the famous spurt and it's Hotbed, half a length in front, Paddyspad then Welcome, Damhead and Birdie Paddyspad challenging for the lead in this four-thousand-pound handicap. . . A kind of deep groaning came from four men's throats. . 'C'mon c'mon c'mon Hotbed c'mon. .' And a counterpoint from Doogle, the manic tin tenor, full of spittle. . 'Paddyspad come on Paddyspad. . .' and then the voice of Arnold, silken with rage in Doogle's ear:

'Make a noise like a betting slip with a hundred and twenty pounds on it you finagling little twerp . . .'

. . and it's Paddyspad the favourite by a neck from Hotbed the outsider that led from the off, Welcome third. .

Left alone by the bar, Doogle searched his pockets for the betting slip, an unconvincing charade, with occasional glances towards the back door.

I'm told there are drowned prisoners in the Dead Sea, preserved by the dense salt, anchored by their legirons, who sway still in the movement of the water, year after year; this is Martin between 'Can I have your glasses please,' and After Time, waiting for strangers to leave.

Four men returned to sit at the table, stiff as Easter Island statues, and as forgiving. A cold murmuring deep-sea quiet as Doogle searched on. . .

'Right. Right then. Mind, I don't know why I'm looking for that betting slip, not a lot of use now is it? Some you win some you lose eh?'

Jack Ledbury leaned forward, abrupt, to stub out a cigarette. Doogle whinnied and dragged out his hands to protect his softer parts. . .

'. . . hahahahaha,' he said, 'I shall have something to say to that feller, he cost me money too you know that? Are we all right for a pint? Did you hear me? I was shouting for the favourite I think, and I can't even remember what it was called. Excitement. I could watch racing just for the racing, me. Are we all having a pint, I'll buy.'

'You better go now Stuart,' said Martin, 'while you've still got the use of your legbones.'

The back door just seemed to flap, and there was no Doogle.

At four pm that afternoon, the pent pressure blew, the table was upturned over a failed bid of two spades, money floated about, voices were raised, and fists. Unfortunately the two policemen who happened to be dozing outside in their squad car were new to the district, and didn't understand. The charges were Drinking After Permitted Hours, Affray, Gaming in a Public Place for Stakes Above the Limit Prescribed by the Gaming Act 1968 As Amended, and Wilful Damage to a Britannia Table. Martin got overexcited and said these police raids were ruining his business, and anyway there wasn't more than a teaspoonful of mild ale between the four glasses so what the hell profit did the officers think there was in that and furthermore it wasn't gaming, it was bridge.

So then he got his for Serving After Hours, and was told that bridge wasn't mentioned in the Gaming Act: they could probably do him for that as well.

I'm not sure if I know where the Floating Bridge Game is now, but I know it's not at the Tinker and Budget.

THE GHOST OF THE MAD
MONK (II)

By the time Bakey had finished, I was good and sick of the Ghost of the Mad Monk. Whatever damn happened, it was the work of the Ghost of the Mad Monk; it's a wonder he didn't use him for an excuse for being late at Assembly, or to get out of the Cross-Country Run. Mind, he's brilliant at giving himself nosebleeds to get out of things, so he didn't need the Mad Monk.

In the Dyeworks, there's this strange small room. It has a door on rollers, that slides open. The wheels it rolls on are still greasy, even though it's never been used for yonks. Inside, there's mysterious packets and big tins, with different coloured powders. You have to be careful how you mess with them, because just a pinch of some of them and your hands or your shirt's marked for life. We got an old envelope once, and I pinched a spoon from home, and took some of the powder out of one of the tins, to see what colour it'd turn out to be. We put a drop, just a tiny bit, in the little dam behind the Dyeworks, and old Clarky saw it when he had us out on a Nature Walk. 'NOTICE HOW THE WATER TURNS GREEN THROUGH THE PRESENCE OF ALGAE CHILDREN,' he shouted at us, 'THIS IS DUE TO THE ACTION OF THE MICRO-ORGANISMS PRESENT IN ALL WATER, AND THE ABSENCE OF OXYGEN IN STILL WATER.' 'It's not Algy,' Bakey muttered to me, 'it's the work of the Ghost of the Mad Monk.' 'SOMETHING AMUSING YOU SON?' Clarky yelled at me. 'It's him,' I said. 'WHO?' he said. 'Him,' I said. Bakey was round the other side of the little dam, I don't know how he got there. I was standing there by myself, like a muffin, and I couldn't get this dopey grin off my face. He must be some kind of a ventriloquist, Bakey, you think he's standing next to you, you're chatting away to him, and then he's somewhere else entirely. 'IT'S NOT YOUR FAULT YOU'RE THE VILLAGE IDIOT I SUPPOSE,' said Clarky, 'BUT YOU COULD MAKE EFFORTS NOT TO LOOK IT.'

Bakey put some of the powder in the lav, after he'd been, and didn't pull the chain. His mother had to stay off work to take him for tests at the hospital. He had to go, in a little bottle, but he couldn't. The next day his father had to have off work to go with him to the hospital. His dad says you go in that bottle, and Bakey said I can't, and his dad said Of Course. Then he went. Naturally it wasn't green. They were baffled. Bakey said they reckoned he had a waterworks disease Unknown to Medical Science, and they'd christened it after him. Oh yes, I said, Bakey's Bladder did they call it? Mad Monk's Waterworks, he said. I'll get him back for that.

We used to be hours in the Dyeworks. Days. I don't know where the time went. It had small old-fashioned windows, and thick cobwebs like raggedy grey blankets. You could imagine yourself in some ancient castle, or else a dungeon. The stone walls were thick, and cold, and wet. Anybody locked away in such a place, they'd never be heard of again. Once, Bakey hid hisself. We'd been poking about in corners, among heaps of rags, in case there was treasure or something, and he'd been saying don't worry if the door clangs shut behind you and you hear the rattle of huge keys and then echoing footsteps departing, leaving you in utter silence. With the rats. Honestly he should get a medal for devotion to TV should Bakey. I'm not bothered, I said, I'd be able to get out of a window. That's right, he said. I looked at the windows. Ten foot from the floor. I'm not bothered, there is no one anyway. That's right, said Bakey, nothing to get worried about is there?

I thought I'll just check if there's stairs down in the next room, or if the windows are lower down. This huge door clanged shut behind me, and then there was a rattle, a few clomp clomp footsteps, and then utter silence. 'Bakey?' I said. Open this door, I said. I wasn't going to try to open it, not me. Pound to a penny he's crept back and slid the bolt back or unlocked it or whatever; I'd push it, and it'd clang open, and there'd be utter silence in the dark room, oh yes, I knew Bakey's tricks. And then after ages, him giving low unearthly moans in a corner, or else leaping out behind me with a wild shriek. 'Bakey!' I said.

I was straining my earballs to hear a noise, any kind of a noise, the scrape of a shoe, breathing. I felt rooted. Then, a bit of a puff, say like a dog snuffling at a door, only loud. You couldn't tell where from, whether it was near, or far off. I listened, holding my breath. Phooooom. Hollow, and echoey. My feet wouldn't move. I could see where there was a door at the other end of the room; there must be stairs down, same as the first room, otherwise why would they have a door in the first place? Where was the noise coming from? Phoooom. It's got to be Bakey, there *is* nobody else. I imagined an owl, big as a mountain, flying silent and low and then its immense cry, filling the air, a dread warning to all living creatures. Its gigantic eyes. Or else a bat. What noise does a giant bat make?

My legs seemed to go strangely weak; I thought I'll sit down a minute. Somehow I ended on my hands and knees on the mucky floor, head bowed down. I thought my mother won't have so much to say about my mucky trousers when she sees the look of frozen terror on my face. There were big cracks between the planks of the floor, and there, right underneath, Bakey. He was bending and holding one of the big glass jars, a hand on either side, and as I watched, he took an enormous breath, blew his lungs up as much as he could, and puffed out across the top of the jar's neck. Phooooom. I thought, I'll strangle him. I'll change my desk at school, I can't stand any more of him. Tell old Clarky my eyes are bad, and I have to sit by a window, my mother'll give me a note. Anyway it's better by the radiator. Mind, he was going to teach me how to do a nosebleed. I'll have to think about it, I thought.

FOR GLADYS

The first time Barry saw Gladys, the wide sky followed a panorama of the village followed the Pennine hills round his head like a kaleidoscope as he spun, went over backwards, and set off down a thirty-degree pitch of Welsh roof slate at gathering speed. He had a hurtling vision of sculptured-gold hair and surprising amounts of porcelain flesh as he thought 'You've always wondered what it was like to fall off a roof,' then every joint jangled as he hit the pile of new-dug earth and venerable sewage beneath. He'll give you quite a good impression of it, with actions, and without prompting: he thinks it was symbolic. Big Jim's about sick of it. I'll tell you why.

Most roofers seem to dislike cat-ladders, they get in the way, but this particular day the roof had been greasy in the morning dew, and Barry had knocked one together from scraps of one-by-one and a plank he'd found, and they'd been stripping the slates and stacking them prior to felting and re-laying. Big Jim happened to be standing on one side of the roof on the ladder, when Barry on the other side had his moment of truth, saw Gladys, felt his feet go from under him, and grabbed for the ridge. His fingers closed over the crosspiece under the end of the plank, which was holding it firm to the roof; the combined weights of Big Jim, and Barry on the crosspiece beat the two nails that were holding the thing together. Barry slithered his way, as Big Jim, cat-ladder and all, tobogganed down the far side; the end of the plank rammed into the guttering, the brackets parted, and the downspouts swayed outwards, until Big Jim was nearly horizontal between roof and gutter, and came to a wavering halt, knuckles white as he gripped the last slates. His bleating obscenities floated from above, but nobody heard, they were busy.

Nobody, not even Barry, was ever sure how many children Gladys had, of her own; she was evasive herself. . . 'Well, this is our Kelly, and our Russell; our Dan and our Douane's at our Doris's. .'; but there were usually between two and five about her, silent, grave, made beautiful beyond their years by missing molars, with sticky pink-striped faces. There were three this time I'm talking about, presumably on a country outing, the girl sucking her thumb, the two boys holding their piggles, clustered round the soft bulk of the woman, concentrated on Barry's meteorite descent, awestruck as he rose again. They could see his mouth moving, but not hear for the clatter of the Hymac that was digging the trench. He was Elvis Presley this week, and the sideburns stood out round his chops, stiff with foul mud. What he was saying was 'What d'you do Saturday nights?'

He tried to take a step, pitched onto his face again. The girl went over for a look. 'Get the site foreman,' he said; 'I've broke me leg I think.' She could hear him close-up. He was suddenly staring grey under the freckles. 'And ask your mam if she'll come and see me in hospital.'

      'Bloody come back here our Tracey you little
      flamer,' said the mother.

Meanwhile the Hymac gave iron tongue at its work of gouging out the sewer trench (you know? – mechanical digger with hydraulic articulated arms, and a huge upside-down scoop at the end? looks even more like a dinosaur than most earth-moving plant does); Kelvin at the levers, his mind mostly on how to get a skipful of the stuff he was shovelling onto his allotment. He'd already had a violent argument with the foreman on misuse of plant and misapplication of diesel. His idea was the machine was standing idle most Sundays. . (MOST? said the foreman, and Kelvin hastened on. .) and and it'd hardly be a pint of diesel between the job and his allotment: there was a mountain of bloody ballast there, said Kelvin, to backfill on top of the new sewer when they'd done. The foreman took this as an aspersion on his ability to order ballast in the right quantity, and yelled, desperate, that he didn't give a damn what the Chinese did with their shit. The other dialogue that was running in Kelvin's mind was what his fellow allotment holders would have to say about this lot when he dumped it; they'd been obstructive about the stuff he got from the mousery; but Kelvin was keen on ecology and re-cycling, and the envious shower of back-biting bastards couldn't argue with his carrots, not for eating or for looking at. It wasn't the smell, he knew that, oh yes, it was the Firsts at the Horticultural. The foreman was in the cabin, eating a biro.

One way or another, Big Jim didn't get much attention, stretched on his isosceles. Brew-time came, Kelvin took his flask back to his van rather than sit in the cabin with the simmering foreman. The foreman wasn't in the cabin, he was outside, waiting for the ambulance. The kids found Big Jim though. They hadn't had such a morning in weeks. They gazed up. 'Hello little children,' said Jim, 'could you tell a man Big Jim wants him?' He smiled then, showing his gums, and the eyes of a hard-pressed stand-up comic; since he only shaves and has his hair trimmed once in a six-month, from below it must have looked like an emotionally disturbed chimpanzee. The ladder was at the far end, where the gutter still held to the wall. The smaller of the two boys climbed one rung, jumped off; climbed two rungs, prepared to jump off.

'GET OFF THAT LADDER YOU
SCABBY LITTLE BRAT,' said Jim.
The boy got off. The ambulance swept up; the driver's
mate got out and looked up.
'Is it you that phoned?' he said.
The ambulance driver's mate told the foreman, when he
found him, that there was a man on a plank on the roof
round the back, shouting; was he all right?
'Be Big Jim, that,' said the foreman; 'he's like a
monkey on a roof.'
'Yes, I can see that,' said the ambulance man.
I think Barry saw himself cradled in Gladys's arms,
saying stoic things, he'd have them ready for sure; but not
even the ambulance men would go near until he'd hopped
clear of the dung, and the foreman had sluiced him with
buckets of water. Barry dragged off his shirt, concentrating on the triceps as he wrung it out, but also giving with
the little crooked Elvis smile. Barry has killer hands, he
says, fairly soon in any new acquaintance. He handed the
shirt to Kelvin. . .
'Better not wring that out any more, or I'll have
it in two halves. Could you give it to my mam
on your way home, and break it to her what
happened? tell her I'm not in any serious pain.'
Gladys had a special china-doll smile on, taking light
secret pleasure in Barry's cockerel-strut, foolish as she
must have known it to be. It was the triceps. Later events
suggest it was also a bachelor's wallet, but that's too simple
a judgement: I never knew a woman so serenely amused
by the antics of men in her presence. .
I have to declare an interest here. My own admiration of
her was like a lover's, in that I thought I detected especial
qualities in her that were hidden from others. Including
Barry. She would give small brief signals of swift intelligence, even wisdom, as if the thick elaborate make-up, the

carefully artificial hairdo, the frivolous clothes, were a conspiracy with me. . or with anyone else she felt well-disposed towards. I passed the side of Barry's mother's house one summer Sunday. Gladys's day. She'd taken off her blouse, and stood, hot and half-naked at the kitchen sink, splashing water over herself. She looked out to me through the window, and then carried on with her business. I felt self-conscious, seedy for looking in, prudish for looking away from someone so well-made. Out of the corner of my eye as I walked on, when I couldn't really see her, not fully, she made a sketch of a gesture, passing her hand across her breasts. For all I know she was brushing off moisture before getting a towel, but in my head it was an act of blessing herself, an acknowledgement, and an acceptance of femaleness. It could well be that I carry an image, an account of Gladys in my mind, like Barry, which is altogether at variance with the objective truth. She had a slaughterman husband, built like a soapstone carving, all heavy grey planes, who knocked her about; you saw bruises on her fragile skin, but her blue eyes never showed a sign of distress, just watchful amusement, as if we were all part of her brood, and would grow up and leave home one day. She tracked down Barry in S1 Ward at the General, picking her way through the labyrinthine hospital bureaucracy without even knowing his name, not bad.

They found Big Jim after the ambulance had gone; Kelvin got him down with the Hymac bucket, plank and all; quite a delicate feat with so heavy-limbed a machine, to grip, lift and lower a sixteen-stone sphere. Big Jim says he knows now how a Praying Mantis feels after his wedding night. Kelvin had to go and sit in his van for a bit. Jim wasn't pleased with any of them, but cheered up when they told him Barry had broken his leg; he'd take him round some Guinness when he'd drawn, Friday. Gladys was already there, in white piqué, stretched tight across her rich curves with never a wrinkle, her delicate round legs crossed, bored bananas. The man in the next bed lay in a rain-forest of drip-tubes, parchment and bone, hardly made a bump under the bedclothes, eyes sunk in brown pits, half-open to examine the ceiling, a slow scan unto death. Barry had already told her about his killer hands, and how he had to restrain his terrible grip with people; he'd fallen back into a troubled reverie about how to do Burt Lancaster with this pilaster of leg strung on wires and pulleys, and in hospital pyjamas. Big Jim opened three cans of Guinness, and his piratical warmth wrapped about the little company. Gladys told them how she'd taken the kids for a picnic out in the country, not far from the site where she'd first seen them, bought some pop and some crisps and some sweets, and having a right good time instead of having to make tea. I don't know, half the human race struggles to feed its children on the best, making sure of the roughage and the protein and the carbohydrates; the other half chucks rubbish down them, and still the children turn out graceful and lively, like small gods.

> '. . . and there was this feller came up,' she was saying, 'all his trousers covered with cow muck and his shirt and in his eyebrows and in his hair. . .'

Her 'e' sounds were nearer the Continental sound, 'ee', so that it came out 'eye-ee-brows' on the strong flow of her narrative, vigorous as the chant of a shaman telling the tribe their myths. . .

> '. . . I could hear him shouting down the field, "Gerroff my land," he shouts, "this is for mowing, for hay." It wasn't,' she said, 'it was just ordinary grass, like in the Park where nobody's wore it out with walking on it; and he

come right up the field to us, and he had all
these flies in his eyes and in his eyebrows and in
his hair. "Gerroff," he says, "this is private."
"All right," I says,' she said, "I will gerroff," I
says, "and the next time I come on," I says,
"I'll bring you a bar o' soap." '

Teeheehee went Big Jim. Barry was wandering in a mist
of love, her chat was wasted on him; the firm column of
her neck, the two fine lines across it, and the little round
bump under her fine-boned chin, smoked his wits; even
the white suit fed his fantasies of hot scuffling in his tent of
linen, wire, pullies and plaster; reality was a long way lost.
The Man in the Next Bed had managed to bring his eyes
round to them, a flicker of rheumy appreciation from deep
in his skull. The Guinness had been stowed in the bedside
locker, next to Gladys.

'Give him a Guinness, Gladys,' said Jim, 'they
allow Guinness in hospital, that's why I brung
it.'

She rose, bunny-dipped in her tight skirt to get a can, bent
forward through the drip tubes to open it in the old man's
sight-line. The froth of her blouse, and the dense pong of
her deodorant seemed to put everything in soft focus; his
pupils grew visibly larger. She held the can for him to sip.
After wetting his lips, he struggled his arms up to rest
himself on his elbows, like an ancient balding rooster, and
Gladys plumped up the heap of pillows behind his
shoulders. He took the can in a blue-veined claw, sipped,
and sank back in an enfolding Nirvana, a dribble of dark
stout at the corner of his mouth, which he sucked back
over the gums.

Big Jim gave Gladys and Barry, at length and in detail,
useful tidbits of gossip, like where building work was
starting, and what the money was like, and who was on
the job, and what he personally thought of each one's

capacities, and his past experience of work, conditions, and worker. They blinked very slowly once or twice during the catalogue, and tried not to look at the clock. Eventually a grateful silence. All three gazed about the ward, looking at other patients and their visitors. Jim noticed the Man in the Next Bed had no visitor.

'All right are you old lad?' he said.

The man held out the can.

'By God he's finished it all,' said Jim. 'Gladys, reach him another.'

She took the empty can and bent, looking about for somewhere to get rid of it.

'What am I supposed to do with this Barry?'

Big Jim and Barry may have heard her, but their attention was entirely taken up with the old man, whose white-tipped fingers stretched through the curtain of tubes towards Gladys's bobbing bum. One of his hands was strapped to a light board, so't he couldn't dislodge the sticking-plaster taping the ends of the drip-feeds to him, but even the pinioned hand was articulating like a pale spider.

'Well I'll just have to put it back among the others,' she said, 'you'll have to watch out you don't knock it over, you'll have drips all over the place. . .'

The old man didn't seem to need support for his back; like a revenant he rose, arms before him, determined, possessed, the tubes tautening; it was as if he was aiming not so much to touch, more to describe the divine shape, religiously and accurately. Others in the ward were breaking off conversations in mid-lump, stopped by the vision of the living dead, rising on a cat's cradle of plastic; the kind of silence you get at the circus, between the drum roll and the death-defying leap. . .

As Gladys finally stowed the empty can, got a fresh one,

and straightened turning with it in her hand, the man had reached his limit, well, everybody's limit really: a well-poised disaster beats bedside chat any time. There was a second's appraisal, then she stepped forward to embrace and rescue him. Her high heel hooked over the leg and wheel of the stand which carried the bottles of drip-feed, pushing it against the iron of the bed as the man plunged forward. Over went stand and bottles, Gladys akimbo between the beds, shrieking with shocked laughter, and the grey body in its winding-sheet nightie cartwheeled onto the cushioning of Gladys in a tangled whirl of skeletal limbs and tufted grey hair. Those who could, stood; the aisle between the rows of beds filled with a squad of nurses, quick-marching like Alpine troops. Swiftly they hoisted him, disentangled his support system, covered him over, and were gone again. Except the Ward Sister, who looked about her with the rage of a betrayed tyrant, face blotchy and pink, a wisp of damp hair across her brow. There's definitely a lump under the bedclothes now, and an expression of peaceful pride on the wasted features. *Nunc dimittis.*

Gladys stood back, hand over her mouth, tears filling her eyes, snorting briefly. She still had the can of Guinness in her hand.

>'Where did that beer come from?' said the Sister.
>
>'I brought it in,' said Big Jim, hasty defender.
>
>'This man is very ill,' she said.
>
>'I think he's improving,' he said.
>
>'Are you telling me he's been given alcohol?' she said.
>
>'Yes,' he said.
>
>'You, are, not, fit, to, be, in, a hospital Ward. Get, out,' she said.
>
>'Look,' said Jim, 'I brought him a dozen

Guinness, that's all.'
'OUT,' she said, 'and don't come back in any
shape or form, ever.'

Back at work after six weeks, Barry would rehearse
Gladys's role to Kelvin in the cabin on wet days or at brew
time. Big Jim refused to listen, read his paper with
ostentatious concentration, rattling it noisily as he turned
the page. Eyes lowered to examine his killer hands, Barry
was solemn:
> 'The thing is, Kelvin, when you truly love
> someone, you respect 'em, and that's something
> you might not understand straight off, and that
> respect mysteriously transforms them, your
> good opinion makes them good. Gladys can do
> no wrong in my eyes. Like with my mam and
> dad. When he was alive. Mind, he was always
> in the boozer, but never a wrong word between
> them. I'm going to kill that bastard husband of
> hers, he'll get his.'
> 'Someone here in love with a married man,'
> said Big Jim, the Problem Page up to his
> nose.
> 'It's a problem that; extra-marital affairs are a
> problem. When me and Gladys are married. . .'
> 'This is a feller that's in love with a married
> man,' said Big Jim.

Barry stopped for a moment over this. Kelvin said he
could do with some downspout offcuts for his leeks.
> 'I've got her a ring,' said Barry, 'but of course
> she can't wear it just yet.'

Barry and Gladys courted like fifteen-year-olds, linking
fingers, self-conscious and rosy with pride in the village
street, sitting ostentatiously one and a half inches apart at

the Bowls Club Saturday night thrash, melded together in a dark corner of the Tinker and Budget in a hot sweet blur of passion, mild ale and Babycham.

> 'Are we going to need a bucket of cold water and a stiff brush?' said Big Jim.

It's fairly pointless to try and conceal your business in a village, social information spreads by osmosis. Maybe garbled, but it spreads. To us at this time, Gladys's husband was one of the scurrying integers we saw from the bus, anonymous, seen once and never again, in the city streets. We were later to discover that this was not how he saw himself, but Gladys seemed to think she turned the corner away from home, and the man no longer existed. Barry on the other hand, brought him to mind once in a while. He surfaced from their pool of sensuality in the pub, and swerved past on his way to the gents. He stopped by me and Big Jim, smacking his fist into the palm of his hand. 'One of these days, that husband of hers is going to turn up,' said Jim. Barry smacked his palm again, and told us he'd never been very good at running away from trouble.

> 'Have you thought you might be carried away from trouble?' said Big Jim, 'on a stretcher.'
> 'It's Gladys's dignity I'm concerned about more than anything,' said Barry, struggling to focus one or the other of his eyes, 'I don't want her mixed up in anything sordid. And she doesn't want it either.'

He swerved on, came to a halt at the back door, and stood, trying to remember why he was there. I caught Gladys's eye.

> 'Other people seem to know better'n me what I want and what I am,' she said, 'so I just lerrum gerron with it.'

Was that it then? A blank? For others to write on? Gladys

powdered her face, sedate; cleaning up the page for further messages, I thought.

Late-night hawkers at both pubs soon learned to make straight for them, and her children would file in out of the night to be loaded with mushrooms, kippers, shrimps, twiglets from the bar for themselves, eggs, 'Uncle Barry'll pay. . . .' Kelvin's allotment had never had such a customer, there were a lot of children. Barry's mother's pension was exhausted on Sunday ham teas, and Barry's wages on taxis to bring Gladys from the gaunt housing estate where she lived. 'Barry'll pay. . .' The Grand Slam was when the phone rang, nine o'clock, Friday night in the Shanter; I answered, it was for Barry: Gladys's sister speaking, they'd booked a minibus from the village taxi service (on Barry's account, I guessed), but there was this club in Oldham with a children's room, so they were there. Would I give him a message to come down, they had an organ? Gladys didn't like to come on the phone herself, in case he'd fallen out with her, but she said to say she'd wait, no matter how long it took him. There was a Chinese takeaway next door to this club. Says Gladys's sister. Barry came in just as I hung up on her rattle; I passed on as much as made sense. I've never seen him so manly. He had on his Sir Francis Chichester rig, yachting cap, blazer, pale blue jeans, but it was definitely Clint Eastwood after he got the phone message: the hands swinging low and loose, the thin hard line of the lips, the narrow gaze across endless dusty grassland, the twitchy crinkle at the corners of his eyes. He caught the Oldham bus.

To me, there was always a blank, alert look about Gladys in company, as if she were looking for clues from Barry as to how he saw her this week, or for satire from his friends. The sleepy watchfulness of a puma in a zoo cage. For all the painful artifice of her shoes, her tight clothes, for all the impositions of her brutish husband (a blackened and bloodshot eye one time, undisguisable), for all Barry's obstinate fantasies, she remained resolutely natural under it all: a strong, healthy, sturdy street arab of a woman. Late one Saturday, outside the chip shop, her rosy mouth opened, and after a hallucinatory delay. . as when a warplane passes, and you get picture before sound. . there came forth her song,

> Just like the ivory
> On the old cottage wall. . .

an ear-rending noise as fearsome as a vixen in heat, nightmare music; every mouth in the chip shop queue was open, every round eye turned to watch it happen, unbelieving. Gladys sang.

A couple of times, her husband came to the village with her; perhaps her renewed radiance after Sunday tea, the stores of perishables the children brought home, the smell of Babycham on Saturdays, alerted him. They would sit together a while at each place where people could conceivably gather; the Park, the two pubs, the Club, the bowling green. . I never saw the man glance at anyone, or look around any more than you would, say, in a city café; and that marked him down for a townee, even if you hadn't known. I had a cockney friend visit once; he was bringing a tray of drinks from the bar into the Tap Room, when he stopped, head down, as if the beer in the pots had suddenly boiled. Then he backed out again. I followed him out.

'Reg? what just happened?'

'Going to be a bundle, ain't there?'

There was, but he was a stranger, knew nothing of our village tensions and antagonisms. I had to suppose a trouble-bone in his head. That was how the slaughterman was. Gladys's eyes would flick from face to face, resting a moment on each, and then on, searching again, I suppose,

75

for clues. Betrayal? None of us even nodded: who could stop Eloïse and Abelard? The allotments was a sociable place the husband missed. That's where Barry was, helping Kelvin to dig over his potato patch. Twice. Barry must have a trouble-bone too.

During the long summer daylight hours of that year of '83, you could hear him, bam bam bam bam bam on a roof of one of the new commuter estates or another, the saw going with Stakhanovite rage, then bam bam bam bam again. . . 'Getting some money behind me.' A thirty-five-year-old bachelor without a ha'penny in the bank, not even a bank account, weekend millionaire, on good tradesman's wages for seventeen years, or else subcontracting on a price; he had glimpsed a dream, and as in dreams, he ran and ran, and never moved forward. I heard wild yells of delighted terror from Gladys's children as Barry played pirates with them among the planks, his fierce roars and barbaric threats. . 'I'll belay your lubbers, aaaah!'. . and then he spun round the corner of a half-built bungalow, clutching his neck and agonizing like Olivier on Bosworth Field, the midget goodies hacking at him with wooden cutlasses he'd made them. Gladys appeared, crisp and clean beyond the mud, and the children departed, quiet as autumn leaves, with money for the shop. Then, it was possible to see that she liked and even admired him, there was a sliver of a chance with Barry, the contrast between this scrawny, tousled, freckled boy/man, and the dangerous bulk of her husband. She would wait for him. Bam bam bam bam bam bam bam. The slaughterman was waiting too, in town.

Barry and Big Jim took a contract with the Council, in town, Kelvin labouring on for them, replacing vandalized doors and windows. The estate had one vast Neapolitan cliff of flats, where the smoke stains of old fires in the rubbish chutes dripped up the walls, a single-storey group of protected housing for old people, with planks nailed across the windows, and some slightly more sane two-storey semi-detached houses, with gardens. It had won a prize for the architect. In South America. For a full morning, they pretended they didn't know it was the estate where Gladys lived. The slaughterman started and finished work early, and weekdays he used the pub on the estate at midday. It was a pub for the desperate, the lads didn't use it, the wired windows and the axe-marks on the doors weren't inviting. They watched the husband's return at closing time, a plastic bag of soft bloody lumps of meat under his arm, his feet piston-style, like a robot, up down, up down, his body rocking forward and then back, so that he didn't seem to swing his legs at all, simply brought them forward into alignment with his body. Never a sign of Gladys. Or maybe a white and golden glimpse on a high balcony, a few jagged shards of song. Barry found it better to start with the back windows, gripped a frame out of Kelvin's van and disappeared round the corner, head down, busy. 'That's one of the little side windows, isn't it?' said Kelvin. Then they saw the husband passing. Big Jim's whiskers were beginning to show tufts of grey; he tugged at them, irritable, looked at the palm of his hand; he used to get compliments on his glossy beard. Kelvin nodded at the husband, 'Howdo.' The man stopped, stared, wooden, at the two strange faces: where had he seen them?

> 'Why cultivate on your face what grows wild on
> your ballbag?' he said to Big Jim, and walked
> on, snickering at his own swift wit.

Eight forty-five in the morning, the children left the flats for the school bus. About ten o'clock, Gladys's sister arrived with several smaller ones, and departed after half an hour or so with more. Barry knew the husband was at work at the Manchester slaughterhouse from five in the

morning. While the others had their snap, he disappeared.
It was inevitable. The sandwiches tasted of nothing in Big
Jim's mouth, the bread dry, and the meat unidentifiable.
Barry was back at two-thirty, refreshed.

> 'Her husband'll take his flaying-knife to you,'
> said Jim.
> 'This is something inevitable,' said Barry, 'don't
> try to interfere.'
> 'You'll be swept away with passion,' said Kelvin,
> 'and not notice the fleeting hours. You'll be just on
> the vinegar-stroke, and he'll be there, looming.'

Barry had the calm indifference to danger of the true
folk-hero.

> 'She sets the alarm-clock,' he said.
> 'Teeheeheeheehee,' said Big Jim.

Whenever the husband was drunk, and they were working
nearby, a foggy recollection would come to him that he'd
seen them before, somewhere, and that it was to do with
his wife. He sought them out a couple of times, and stood
in the road, at a distance, puzzling at it. In the end I
suppose he had a clearer memory of having seen them
there at work than the brief time he'd glimpsed them on
their home ground. He spoke to Kelvin once.

> 'Can you imagine what it's like for a husband
> and a father not to know the true mind of his
> wife and the mother of his children?'
> 'Aye, you're right there, mate,' said Kelvin.

Barry was on the other side of the garden, his bootlaces
had come undone, and the light was better there.

> 'They pick the flowers,' said the slaughterman,
> 'but they don't cultivate the plants.'

It was going to happen. It had to happen. The way it
happened was this. . .

The lads were working on another estate, about a mile from Gladys's; Barry continued to keep his midday trysts, back dead on two-thirty. Bank Holidays don't make a lot of difference to contract building workers. In fact they hardly noticed it was a Bank Holiday, until Barry had departed for his working lunch.

'What time the pubs shut Jim?' said Kelvin, 'Sunday hours is it?'

Big Jim stopped chewing his sandwiches, he thought he'd concentrate on swallowing for a bit. Kelvin was watching his face carefully as he continued his light chat. . .

'Dinner time I mean; two o'clock is it, Bank Holidays?'

The husband would be home early, sober.

'We're his mates,' said Kelvin; 'I know he said not to interfere and all that, but I'd like to know what happens, wouldn't you?'

He said he had some bedding plants in the back of the van, they could take a tray of them and go up to the flat, and they could knock on the door, and they could say the Council wants tenants to Keep Britain Beautiful, and would they like some plants for window boxes eh? Lobelia he had, from seed, they were for a mate, he said. Big Jim said was Kelvin always such a pimple-brained pillock, or had he been on a special course?

Sections of what happened next in Gladys's flat have kept a frozen clarity in Barry's mind ever since, although he can hardly be brought to speak of it. The time-scale, on the other hand, is warped: sometimes seconds took days to go by, sometimes minutes shrivelled into micro-seconds. The front door clicked open, and heavy footsteps shuffled in the hallway, a jacket rustled. The husband's breathing was loud in the flat. The adrenalin raging round Barry and Gladys made breathing redundant. He wrestled into pants, jeans, shirt (he found he still had his socks on, he's as fast in forward as he is in reverse); he managed to mouth 'Is there a fire escape?' He knew there was only one way to the front door, and he knew who was in it, coming this way, filling the space, wall to wall. Gladys had got into her coat-dress, and sat on the bed, buttoning with fingers too hot for efficiency; she shook her head among damp curls of hair, nodded towards the windows. On the balcony, he straightened, the far purple horizon of his own friendly hills seemed to tilt, his neighbours there didn't take huge knives and do things to people they hardly knew; he looked along to the next balcony, a mere four feet away, the crumbling parapet, the five-storey drop beneath, he was back in the room. He gulped to control his breathing, achieving a low airless groan; Gladys closed her eyes tight, her lips drawn back from pink-stained teeth. From the living room, the stone silence of a man who listens. When she opened her eyes again and grabbed for her knickers among scattered frillies, they disappeared simultaneously: Barry's hand from under the bed scooped all the underwear out of sight. Disorientating, but it made a kind of bizarre sense, and then his boots were dragged in after. She had the impression of a brightly coloured Giant Tortoise, retracting under threat.

Big Jim and Kelvin reached the sixth floor, and leaned against the wall till the dizziness went. Kelvin held the tray of bedding plants before him like a flag-seller. It didn't seem all that convincing a front any more; even the prospect of seeing Barry make an unscheduled flight through a closed door wasn't thrilling now. The lift, jammed permanently at this floor, gaped before them like an ante-room to hell, scorched and scrawled on by the damned, a heavy stench of dog muck. Jim looked down the stairwell, worked out how many turns they'd made on the way up, checked that it was indeed the sixth floor (it was painted large on the bare concrete, and all the numbers began with 6, but Jim's world was filling with uncertainty and doubt); he satisfied himself with his calculations, and nodded towards the right-hand side of the corridor.

'Be that side, 'bout three or four doors along.'

'We'll need to listen a bit, check on what's going on in there, thuds and that, or screams, before we make our move Jim. He may be being held against his will.'

'Did you bring the stun grenades?' said Big Jim, bitter.

Within the bedroom of the flat, the space between the sagging hessian of the double divan bed and the fluff of the rubber-backed carpet was not big; Barry's head was pressed, squidged, pummelled by aged springs, as husband and wife improved the hot Bank Holiday after-noon, at length. On and on it went, dummadummadum-madummadummadummadumma. . . His killer hands squeeze his cheeks as he tells it, the eyes start with remembered disbelief and anguish, the lips trumpeting soundless grief. . . dummadummadummadumma-dumma. . he would have covered his ears, but his head was sideweays squashed, he would have fled, reckless, but the bed gripped him as no bed has ever gripped a man, dummadummadummadummadummadummadum-madummadumma. . . . he heard every last incoherent eloquent syllable, the rust dusting down into his eyes and ear, the sneeze rising peaking, about to detonate in him. . and then the fart, the dreadful rending fart and the racked lover praying that it was his own and then not praying that and certainly not sneezing: *whose was it?*

Finishing with a speaking pause, a huge heave and settle, and the husband's mumbled. . .

'Like a billposter's bucket,'

the slowing of the breathing, grading into small rasps of

snores, lips smacking, spaced, comfortable. There's reasons for believing, with proof, that the whole grisly business took less than fifteen minutes; for Barry, it was a lifetime, his lifetime: he was a very much older man after this. Then the deep sonorous wind-tunnel roar of Fingal's Cave snores; he imagined towering ocean waves at long intervals, destroying and being destroyed by rocks. His fingers closed again on boots. He edged and squeezed his sweat-soaked, cramp-ridden body towards the dim light of the room, shouldering up the frame of the bed for the extra eighth of an inch he needed to escape, ears alive for the slightest variation in the storm of snores. . .

The alarm-clock went off. Fixed, transfixed, crucified by the frame of the bed as the slaughterman's hand reached out for the bedside cabinet, dobbed about till it found the clock, turned it off. The two thick legs thumped down before his eyes. A smell of feet like a charnel house. The husband dressed, stolid. His hand groped again at the cabinet top, scratch scratch, gave up; a jingle as he found keys and money in his trousers pocket. . .

'See you dinnertime love,' said the husband, and left.

A sleepy mutter from the wife as she turned over.

Kelvin straightened from the letterbox as the husband emerged, jacket in hand. The man bustled on, bleary, stopped. Returned for a look: where in the name of Jesus had he seen them before? It was Kelvin who spoke.

'I think we must of got the wrong flat.'

'What wrong flat?' said the man.

'That one, number 6030, it's the wrong one.'

'So what you telling me for?'

'You seemed to be interested. We're just Making Britain Beautiful.'

The flat door opened, and Barry's right eye, pink with the

salt sweat, peeked out at them from behind the slaughter-man. Without looking back, the man gripped the tag on the lock, and tugged it closed again, aware that something was tightening tension in Kelvin in front of him. The husband had suspicions; the men were clustering closer round his marital home; wherever he looked, things changed, reality altered.

'What time is it?' he said.

'Two twenty-nine,' said Kelvin.

'Two twenty-nine. Two twenty-nine when?'

'Two twenty-nine now. Well, two-thirty.'

'In the morning? You're making Britain beautiful at two thirty in the morning?'

Kelvin felt himself being sucked into a shared insanity, he doubted his watch, he doubted the lobelias; he appealed to Big Jim.

'It's not morning is it? it was daylight when we came in wasn't it? It's afternoon isn't it?'

The next door along the corridor opened, and Barry slid out, boots in hand, the somnambulist; he walked away from the little group, towards the further exit stairs, steady and unseeing.

'That feller'll know,' said Kelvin.

'What will he know?'

'Whether it's the right flat.'

'It's not the right flat.'

'The Council could've got it wrong eh?'

Kelvin, with the tray of bedding plants before him, and Big Jim in a humble queue behind, eased past the slaughterman in the direction of their departing friend. Barry was accelerating, though the acceleration was so gradual only his panic-stiffened back betrayed him.

'. . and he'll know what time it is, you'll have to excuse us. . .'

Kelvin was away, the rattle of his footsteps on the concrete giving extra charge to Barry; Big Jim squeezed by, holding in his belly, nodded at the man, affable:

'We were just looking for a friend,' he said.

'You haven't found one,' said the man. Self-pity welled up in him; his father had been funny in the head long before old age; the Magistrate had said he needed help an' all. 'I don't know whether it's day or night,' he said.

'It does happen,' said Big Jim.

'My knives are in my locker at work,' said the man, 'but if you give me decent notice before you come round again, I'll geld the pair of you.'

Two pairs of boots behind him in the corridor and then down the stairs – Barry hoped it was two, not one, but he made good speed. It surprised neither of his friends when they got in the van and Barry rose from among the shovels and bags of cement and planks in the back.

'He got me at a disadvantage,' said Barry, 'no boots on. Soon as I find out which pub he uses, I'm having him.'

'He uses the Snipe, on the estate here,' said Kelvin.

'When I see Gladys Sat'day night,' said Barry, 'I'm definitely having it out with her what she did to me.'

'Stop this motor,' said Big Jim, 'I want to strike him.'

'I don't think I should,' said Kelvin. 'Are we coming round to the Snipe tonight? I dare say he'll be in. I'd like to see the finish of it.'

'Ah, well, well he'll be among his friends there,' said Barry, 'but I'll find him, wherever he is. He'll get his.'

I think that's Sinatra is it? You know better when he's got the hat on, and the raincoat over his shoulders.

84

GONE AWAY

Some stories, you piece together. The Sowerby house stands empty now, grimy lace curtain at one of the lower windows. The moor rises at the back, you can see into the small back bedroom: chest of drawers, split across the top, not worth taking away, Victorian swing mirror on it. . 'Very old, you'd get pounds for it,' . . old equals valuable in these hills. . they'd left it. A dead house-martin between the sashes of the window, mummified by sun and the dryness of the house. Derek's room. A few raggedy sheep in the little meadow, the walls broken, no Derek to keep them sound.

The simplest, most direct of men, he told me as we waited for the bus together how every time he made up his mind to go into town, he'd get ready in his room: 'So's she wouldn't find me another job to do.' She'd give him money, but every time and only at the last moment: it drove him crackers. Always neat for his excursions, it was easy to imagine him scrubbing his fair stiff hair flat, long grey raincoat belted ready for out; peering at the speckled mirror through glasses so thick his eyes swim like oysters behind them; mother at the sink, radio tinkling weakly.

Always the radio at that house, never seemed to have a decent battery in it.

> 'That you our Derek? Don't think I don't know
> what you're up to in the bedroom!'

Her antennae wick to every creak, every quiet movement; who else would it be in his bedroom? He could keep his shoes off till the last moment, no good. She was waiting at the side door; he could see the money, peeping out between finger and thumb. A quick, rough embrace, pressing him to her with a strong arm, his nervous evasion making it more like a headlock. Kissed him, put on a stern expression, eyes examining every detail of his face, as if it were for the last time.

'Well, you're off out. You can do, there's
nothing to keep you here.'

She drew in her breath, one last chance to hold him. Phrases passing slowly round her head, jostling, edgy, she tried them at random. Derek's account of it a convincing mimicry of a mind where intentions and words don't marry.

'I'll just ask you to bear in mind, a family holds
to what it's got.' Fished again at phrases, tight-
lipped, uncertain: 'This place'll be worth a lot
of money in due course; I shan't always be
here.'

'I'm in a hurry Mam.' Surely she'd give him the
money? he clenched his fists, he'd be throttling
her next.

'I'll be in my bed by the time you're back; you
needn't concern yourself with me.'

Her eyes to the kitchen, where the father sat, stolid over the newspaper. Derek could smell the closeness of her, mild, thick, like a cow's breath, not the sharp rank smell of his father.

'Yes, Mam.'

'There's a future for everyone, we've got to look
to it.'

'I don't understand what you're saying Mam.'

'I've a lot on my mind.'

The small, neatly folded wad of notes, pushed into his hand.

'You get nothing for nothing in town. Let's see you put it in your purse.'

He trudged the long rough lane, towards the main road down into Ravensgill. His mother on the doorstep, dour, bereft.

'Mind you catch the ten past ten back!'

He pulled one hand out of his raincoat pocket, raised it, cupped, in acknowledgement, not looking back. Hastened his pace.

'D'you hear what I say?'

Her figure smaller now as he turned onto the road, no other lights on the hillside. The father coming out, buttoning his railwayman's jacket, stuffing snap-tin into the pocket, flask; switched on the ignition of his autocycle, the headlight cutting the dark. Their conversation clear in the still night air, miniaturized by distance, blurred by the occasional passing car.

'You're off early.'

'Yes.'

'I know what he goes for. He's been on edge for ten days or more, so I've been on the watch-out, making sure he's got jobs to do. But you can't argue, he's grown, and that's it.'

'I've said that all along, but you wouldn't listen.'

'He works hard, he needs his rest, he's in the fields all hours.'

'He needs time off in lieu as well.'

'You're a fine one to talk, when did you last have time off?'

He fiddled with the controls of the bike, uncertain at first, easing by loose stones, whined off up the lane. She stared into the night, bewildered. Always, when Derek was away, the dissolved distress of a small girl, the future washed away. She spoke one time of his three days in hospital, when he was nineteen, as if I could open a book and explain the world to her:

'I don't know what I'm going to do.'

At the bus stop, Derek spoke guilelessly of his mother's manoeuvres. Perhaps encouraged by my amused complicity, he went on to tell how he'd got on on a previous town trip, taking no account of Mrs Whitehead, coming for the same bus, except to greet her cheerfully.

'This woman was taking off all her clothes in the room. She said you take your clothes off and be in the bed ready. Drops her little dainties off one by one, into the bottom drawer of this chest. I was getting excited. Then she says hold on, I'll just have to go to the bathroom. I waited and waited. In the end I got up and had a look. There was no bathroom; I went back and pulled out the drawer; it was empty, no bottom in it; her clothes must have fallen through to the room underneath when she closed it. When I got downstairs, I could see there was this hole in the ceiling; no sign of her. Ten pound she had off me.'

He grinned, holding his purse up by his nose to be able to see in clearly, fishing out change for the fare among clean notes.

'Did you tell your mother what happened?'

Side on, you can see his eyes, lashes almost white, vulnerable; he closed them, secret:

'No-ooo.'

He seemed to relish the experience, it made him matter perhaps, he had something to say about himself that was of interest. Mrs Whitehead in the bus shelter looked anywhere but at us, her eyes merry, her lips compressed.

'Mam says to watch out with women, they let you down,' he said, 'so I watch out with her.'

My walk takes me by the Sowerby house often enough: neat, with a town look about it, whereas many isolated dwellings in the hills go unpainted. Across the fields, a group of farm-buildings that have been modernized: limestone ballast track up to the crisp new gate, white-painted barge-boards on the gables, rows of small windows framed with weatherproofed timber, autumnal Laura Ashley print curtains. No farmer in this house: Con's house; her husband Laurie set her there, worked as long as daylight and weather would let him, until it was right, put his tools and paint-pots into an outhouse 'for ever', and then went back to the oil rigs, Saudi, Ghana, even Australia. Three-month contracts, good money, irresistible, one-month leaves, serene honeymoons every time, he used his youth while it was there; Con's, he seemed to think, was there for ever.

She stood by the gate, looking out over the valley, a foolish red setter her only company; the dog whined, back up, barked, panicky, weaving about until she set her hand on it. My own dog stiff-legged on the other verge. Long black hair, streaked with rare silver, face ivory, as if carved, in firm lines, the brow and nostrils finely arched, movements easy and athletic. . she'd shared her husband's passion for rock-climbing; Norwegian born, I think. I said good morning; a smile moved the corners of her mouth, just, and she lowered her eyes, as if she'd got out of the habit of speech. When Laurie's home you see them out for a meal in a moorland pub, visiting old climbing friends, her dark eyes taking everything in, greedily, restless as a child, talking, talking, gathering up the gossip of months, Laurie's adventures. Laurie slamming the car door, attentive to her, proud, hastening in after her.

I coincided with her one evening at the Motel. Bolt upright on her stool, a tall glass in front of her; caught her eye as I eased in to the bar, her pupils huge, unfocused.

She left almost at once, the drink half-finished. Her comfortable walk was a treat in itself. I rested my hand on her stool, the thick cloth was sodden and warm. Too lonely to go out without being pissed? too shy and too pissed to talk when she's out? phew. Loneliness closes in on you, I know that. Though some seem to choose it, embrace it. Laurie was one such. Her calm good looks made her self-assured in her husband's eyes, I suppose. But I don't think she was.

Laurie soon recognized how useful Derek could be; his deft skill and strength were apparent: Derek picked up a stone for a wall, and placed it, once, it would be there for a hundred years. A strange conversation with Mrs Sowerby, who could not refuse, as she would have refused people she knew, out of well-founded mistrust, old grudges. Laurie thought rum turkey, his words.

> 'I wonder if your son could do us a favour? I'd pay him of course, cash in the hand: three pounds suit?'

She waited for him to state his business; this sunburnt stranger, red track suit, picked out in brilliant white, spotless trainers, who talked easily of money, making her uneasy with other manners, other customs, than the self-interested and abrupt ways she was used to.

> 'They come by,' she said, 'they'll say that gate of yours is buggered; I've got a gate, they'll say, handy. Oh yes, everything for favours and thank yous. Next minute they're round for eggs, and then it's a roll of wire.'

She stood at the door, the wind plucking at her flimsy stained pinafore, stockings rolled down from doughy marbled legs, one hair slide holding her short straight hair. The new neighbour seemed cleaner than other people she knew, mint bright: why would anyone dress like that? what to do? Mr Sowerby behind her, an uncertain smile, an abstracted 'u', not mirthful or friendly. Laurie tried again.

'We've got a bit of wall down.'

'I know.'

'I've seen his walling on your land, any chance he could come over and help us out? I thought three pounds an hour. . .?'

Laurie marvelled at his own nonsense, applying to Mrs Sowerby as if Derek were a schoolboy, and the father a deaf mute: he erased the smile. Mrs Sowerby was talking.

'I'll want to see the money here. He's a good worker, he *has* worked, folks'd take advantage. He'll be down nine tomorrow, he has the hens to see to before anything.'

Laurie could see she was gasping, pressing her lips together, her colourless eyes staring at him. Her words came in gabbled bursts.

'In fact he's enough to do and more. Without going outside of here. I don't want him going outside of here. It'll be sheep-dipping next, and no dog to help. I can see where that wall's down. And I can see it from the window too. I'll have my eyes open.'

She should have known, she did know, it was a warning, but she couldn't read the hectic message her pulse tapped out. Laurie heard the husband as he left, caught a glimpse through the window of the face, smiling broadly in fury:

'Where do they come from? we don't know that; what kin have they? They've no beasts on, what do they want walls for? I don't know why they came here, we're all right as we are.'

The woman's dismissive mumble; the man's voice rising, knowing she hardly listened:

'You never listen!'

Derek turned up the next morning; six foot of wall was

rebuilt by midday; Laurie paid him, nine pounds. Around twelve pounds a square yard at that time, to get a firm in, for drystone. Mrs Sowerby had to wait till Derek came home before she saw the money, Laurie ignored that part of the deal; he could see it wouldn't take much to find himself falling out with the mother, and he wouldn't know what it was about. Con laughed, light, brief, and he didn't know what that was about either.

And there were other jobs. Once the place was finished, Laurie had better things to do on his home leaves. A drainage channel for the driveway; get Derek to do it. Barn door hinges resetting; get Derek to do it; you ask him Con, it pleases him if you ask him. Mind you pay him cash, plastic money hasn't come to the hills yet. As the days lengthened, Derek stripped to his shirt, the long flat muscles jumping. For a while, Mrs Sowerby would come to the road, strained, if the work took him out of sight, but even she got used to Derek coming and going; nothing was neglected, Derek wasn't altered, he went into town once in a while, came back on the ten past ten, grinning to himself; father and son framed in the barn door, dust and sunshine, sweating and wordless as they sheared, the high metal drone of the shears, two of them to hold the old tup, thirty-five fleeces, the money banked, by the mother. He was so ordinary, it was so ordinary, the steady figure moving about the paddock, two-pound mason's hammer for every job, be it stone work or fencing. Con graceful in the long exotic dresses Laurie brought home, silk, bright tropical prints, quilted jackets, bringing a mug of tea to the worker, the handsome glossy dog gambolling free: Derek's friends. Con's door open on the fresh upland weather of summer, as was Mrs Sowerby's. Most of Derek's work on their own holding, just odd jobs for Con. A landscape with figures, high vapour trails, the dark edge of the moor, the bright farm buildings and fences, suspended in slow movement till Laurie came home, the leaden surface of the reservoir below, anglers about it, dreaming into autumn.

And then, the figures taken out, the doors closed, the trout season over.

Laurie came home after three months, paid off the taxi at the lane end, looked about him. Starlings rose in a cloud as the car turned back on the main road. The farmhouse door would open now. He breathed deep, stretched his legs, reached the yard.

'Con? Hallo!'

Silence, except for the distant woosh of heavy wagons. Must be shopping; no, her little Beetle still in the barn. Damn dog, only barks at hikers and the postman. Can a dog be trained to bark at the right people? He thrust both hands in his pockets for the key. . where the hell? There was one under a little flagstone he remembered. Had he written the wrong date? His airmail letter of a fortnight ago lay among circulars and bills behind the door. Dazed by incomprehension, he went to the kitchen. Cup, saucer, mug, plate, knife, spoon on the draining board, washed, a faint fine dust over them. Bed made. Wrenched open the door of the long bedroom cupboard, packed with dresses, coats, didn't make sense. The fridge then: full. Milk, sour.

On the phone to Harry Mooney at the Police House, he strained for an even tone, keep to the facts, ice in his stomach.

'I'm at home, Con's not here. And her car is. Have you seen her?'

'Not for a while, but she's not much about when you're away. I might see her shopping in the village, but I'm not always on, Thursdays. Have you talked to the Sowerbys?'

'No, we hardly have any acquaintance with

them; Derek does the odd job, that's all.'
'I've seen him about your place.'
'Harry, the dog's not here.' He scrubbed his
face with his free hand, looked at it trembling,
clenched it.
'Well that's it then, she's taken the dog for a
walk.'
'There's a letter of mine on the mat here, must
have been here a week at least.'
A pause.
'Laurie, she's a grown-up girl.'
'That's it then is it?'
His own voice sounded tinny to him, as if he was listening
to it on the phone; Harry relented.
'I'll come up. But have a word with the
Sowerbys will you? What about family?'
'She's got a sister in Kendal. That's all. Parents
lived in Oslo. There's cousins, but we aren't big
on letters. Cards at Christmas, that's all.'
He had no order for his thoughts; he imagined Harry,
with his notebook mind, waiting for concrete information,
and all Laurie's mind would give him was a sum that didn't
add up.
'Her parents are dead; did I say that?'
'I'll finish my tea, then I'll be up.'
Mrs Sowerby barely opened the door, her face obstinate, enclosed. Derek at the table, didn't look round. He
wouldn't be coming round over any more jobs, she said,
he'd enough to do without that. She was getting on now,
she needed her son about her, not gadding off. No, she
hadn't seen the lady; couldn't say for how long. While ago.
Derek spoke, hunched over bread and jam.
'She said she'd be going away for a bit.'
'When?'
'While ago.'

'Couldn't you be more specific?'

Mrs Sowerby closed the door. He should have been more neighbourly in the past, but they weren't easy people; like talking to Abos, he told Harry later, you couldn't read the expression, their experience was a blank to him.

He made Harry come with him to the barn. To one side, a soft, dented cushion of hay left by the previous owners. Harry bent casually, to turn it over, not making too much of it; the fragrance rose in the still air. They looked in outhouses. Was there anything missing? clothes? suit-cases? How the hell would he know about clothes? Suit-cases, yes, that's a thought. Laurie ran upstairs, the long cupboard, top shelf. The full set of suitcases was there, wedding present, he knew them, no mistake, only the battered one he used himself was missing, downstairs. The hallstand. Harry held out Con's shoulder bag; Laurie pulled out her purse, checked inside, stupefied: how had he missed it? Credit card, cheque book, *keys*. He leaned, one hand on the newel post, chest heaving. Held his brow between finger and thumb, shaking his head from side to side, as if thoughts were foul flies about him.

> 'Harry, she's bloody gone mate; she's not just away for a bit.'
> 'Yes, it has a look of that; I'll report her missing. D'you have a photograph? By the way, what happened to the dog?'

Together, they searched every room, not looking at each other as they opened cupboards, crouched to see and to grope under beds. Harry went, and he was alone. Her sister came, but there wasn't much to say. Con was always the unpredictable one. Would you like a cup of tea? She went home, to her children. The police came, their voices, questions, echoing as if there were no furniture in the room; were he and his wife on good terms? Cadets, fanning out over the fields, earnest and concentrated, eyes

down, loud-hailer marshalling them. Dogs, leaning on
their leashes, criss-crossing, quartering the ground; men
in black raincoats, easing their bulk into the Sowerby
doorway, emerging expressionless, raising a hand in
formal goodbye, not looking back. And then they were
gone again, and the total silence of the house descended on
him.

    'Con?'

He didn't eat enough, he knew, his tan grew yellow as he
paled beneath it, sitting in the house, listening to endless,
mindless music. Forced stale biscuits on himself, ate
cheese from the plastic wrapping, tasteless from the
fridge, biting off lumps, hands trembling. One day a
ferocious storm beat across the valley, thunder cracking
below the house; he watched the rain gusting against the
windows as if thrown by the bucketful. After eight days,
there was nothing to eat.

    'Con?'

He pulled on his anorak, climbing boots; the hall mirror
showed him they looked a bit rum over his crumpled
mucky tracksuit, but he had to get out, now; the house was
a prison, indifferent, having no meaning; Con's absence
emptied the place, the clinical white walls were a punishment, shadowless. What the devil had he been thinking of
to leave her here? *keeping* her? like a pet? an ornament?
They were independent, they'd said, no ties, no questions
when he came home.

    The Waterman stopped his Landrover by him on the
road to the village.

    'I was coming to see you. We've had the leaflet.'
He showed it to Laurie: Con's serene face, big knitted
bobble hat, pulled well down at the back. He remembered
it blue. On Dovestones, an icy day.

    'It says there was a red setter.'
Laurie nodded, avoiding the leaflet.

'There's a dog in the reeds, where we've been
draining. I thought it'd been shot, sheep-
worrying. I was coming back to it when the job
was done: the crows clean 'em up pretty fast. I
had another look this morning, after we got the
leaflet. There's not a mark on it.'

The man chattered as they plodged through the stale
marsh water, bright orange in places. Laurie's mind filled
in the photo, her gaiety in the company, and the effort of
the climb, the curses at danger, the towering gables of
rock. He tried to organize his thoughts for Harry later, and
for himself. What had he ever done but make her the
reflection of his own efforts? what had she ever asked? the
house was his notion, she was perfectly content with the
small town terraced house; he poured all his earnings and
all his efforts into that goddam farm, because it was near
the rockfaces, they'd agreed on it, well, she hadn't objec-
ted, and then he went. And now she'd gone. The dread of
loving ached in him, not the loss, or the need. Where?
where? where? It was like when you try to write a letter,
and you've nothing to say. The Waterman had stopped,
and was staring at him, hostile:

'I told you,' he said, 'in the reeds. How d'you
mean "where"?'

'I don't know my own wife.'

'Who does?'

'We had that rainstorm, could have washed it
out, there's a culvert. A dog'll crawl into a
corner to die. The police looked. Mind, I don't
suppose they were really looking for a dog.'

The Waterman fell silent, reflecting on what he'd said.

It lay on a hummock, where they'd pulled it; the
beautiful coat matted, streaked, parted by water, showing
a dead, potato-coloured skin. The magpies had already
taken the eye from the side he could see. A vigorous flow of

pellucid water from the culvert, over sand washed silver. Heaps of weeds and mud where the men had been clearing the drainage. And two old pennies, big, clean and clear, mint condition, 1949. Who would carry two old pennies about to drop them? For some reason, Laurie's mind and heart contracted more over the coins than over the sad corpse of the dog. Why here? Both 1949? He showed them to Harry, who put them in an envelope, solemn, and said he'd tell the detective inspector in charge. The D.I. told Harry piss off, he'd enough on his mind.

A warrant was sworn, and Derek brought in. It was the only thing that made sense: the dog set strangers, even the postman, it wouldn't have gone away from the house unless it had been with someone it knew and trusted. The few friends who had called by to see Con had been in company, and had been reluctant to hang around with their friends till she came home, they'd left. They were accounted for. The only words Derek responded to were the sergeant's 'You have no need to say anything. . .' He cocked his head, nodded briefly. After that, random remarks, making little connection with the questioning. He was worried who was looking after the hens. Laurie had been good to him and his mam. And Con had too. The detectives spent four hours in relays with him, went off duty no better informed than when they arrived. When did he last see Con? Who else could have taken the dog away from the house? What was the last job she asked him to do? Had she dismissed him? The same questions, round and round, they couldn't think of any other way to come at him. One of them bullied him, shouted at him, angry, his face twisted down into Derek's:

> 'Simple are you? some kind of idiot? what happened between you two eh? she wouldn't have anything to do with a little craphead like you eh? that it? Christ you stink!'

His heavy hand smacked into the averted face, the glasses dislodged from one ear, then dropping down his front. Derek sat at the table, one fist clutching the other, pressing down on the clean wad of paper.

'She said she'd be going away for a bit.'

The detective hurled himself out of the room, slammed the door. Harry Mooney was at the filing cabinet, the exiguous case evidence on the top, search report, notebook of dates, sketch plans of farmhouse, area, the culvert, map marked with thick red crosses and circles, all neatly enveloped and labelled; the two pennies lay in his hand; as the detective came out, he dropped them back in their envelope, shoved everything hastily back in the file and into the cabinet. The detective muttered at him, vindictive:

'We're going to have to let the little bastard go. He's got the Wall of China round his head. No evidence, bar a dead dog, no body, no talk in the village, no sign of a break-in, the Sowerbys saw nothing. Or they saw everything. What a bunch of prunes we look. It's not some anonymous city job this, none of your assailant disappearing in the crowd: everyone *knows* this hillbilly, *everybody knows* he's a randy little git. Woman vanishes, dog dead. We have the only mortal person who could possibly have anything to do with it, and he's going to walk out of here in half a pissin' hour.'

He wiped his mouth with the heel of his hand, there were bubbles of spit.

'Hick,' he said.

Harry took in a mug of tea, and set it down on the table. It occurred to him that in all the time he'd known Derek, he'd never seen him without the glasses muddling his face. It was a good strong face, brow furrowed, a square jaw, slightly underhung. Harry had a sudden cold notion of what Derek would look like and represented to a lonely woman.

> 'She said she'd be going away for a bit. When she came back, her husband would be due home, she said, and we weren't to have nothing no more to do with each other.'

Harry stood, motionless, arrested in mid-pace on his way to the door, his eyes on the floor, listening, intent.

> 'She wasn't like other women. She was be-yutiful, smelt be-yutiful. When Mam took me into her bed, I used to like it, it eased me; she could see that I was badly, and she helped me because she's my mam.'

Harry turned back to look at Derek, blinking slowly, concentrated. Derek sniggered, furtive, a quiet, barley sugar gurgle. Then anxious pain round his bleached eyes.

> 'And then when she started giving me money for women, I could feel better in myself, and not angry, but they weren't loving with me. When I was there, I could understand everything. Clouds, everything. She knew names for 'em. I know what they're going to do, but not names. Work was nice when I did it for her. And when she said that. . and when she said that. . .'

His voice wandered unsteadily into a groan of pain; he swallowed, reached for the mug of tea, held it in both hands, as if to warm himself. He looked round for Harry, screwed up an eye at the dark blur between him and the door, turned away again.

> 'That was the most she ever talked to me, except do this and do that; and was I all right. She said to tidy away the hay, we'd have no further use for that. Speaking very quiet, and

serious. I put my arms round her. I'd never done that before without she showed me she wanted me to. She struggled a bit, shaking her head. Her hair was getting wet. She used to lean her head back, but she wouldn't now, she said "no", and "no more". I tried to push her head back, the way she did it before. She said "no". Her breath smelt strange, like pubs; but like scent too. I couldn't understand scent on her breath. Then she stopped struggling. It was a good while I think. Very soft. Her eyes were open. I closed them, like my mam did with grandma. I knew what to do. I told my mam what I'd done. She said to get her into a cornbag. It took two, I had to go back for another. That night she'd gone stiff. We took her up over the moor, and mam made me dig into the peat to cover her over, and then draw the bags over where we'd trodden; I was glad when the chandler came for 'em. It's a place where hikers don't go by, but I know it well enough, you get sheep sheltering there the odd time; nuisance they are, 'cause they get bogged down. It's a long way up there. I drownt the dog the same night. In the reservoy. Mam said to do that. And hide it after.'

Mrs Sowerby was put on probation; presumably on a promise not to do it again. During the trial, his father brought a petition round to sign, still the same u-shaped humourless smile. I saw his mother shopping, greeted her. She stopped, sudden, looking at me sideways, pale plump face pursed up, searching my face for. . disapproval? judgement? I felt none. A brief image of her taking Derek into her bed, one body taut, coiled, the other reasty with bad feeding, slack; one mind straightforward as a

beast in the field, the other anxious as an old hen. Then
Derek dreamed his nightmare.

'He worked hard,' she said, 'I've nobody to look
to now.'

'I'm sorry,' I said.

'You have to be poking in where you're not
wanted don't you?' she said. 'Worse nor a
policeman, everlasting round the place, I've
seen you. Well you see the results I hope?'

Derek got life.

I talked with Harry about it, much later, wondering
why Derek had ever confessed; he must have heard the
detective cursing and saying they'd have to let him go
surely? Laurie was across the road by the newsagent's, in
Con's Beetle, his friendship with Harry demolished by the
evidence Harry had had to give.

'You'd have to guess at that,' said Harry, 'Derek
wouldn't tell you, even if he had any notion.

You know those two old pennies we found?'

I'd heard, from Laurie.

'Did you know they were both 1949?'

I didn't see any consequence. He turned to look me in the
face:

'That was the year Derek was born.'

I held my breath, paralysed, without any feeling of
where I was. Harry resumed his copper's survey of the
passing scene. .

'Would you say they'd had them on one side for
their own laying-out up there?'

A young woman came out of the shop and got into the
Beetle with Laurie; he looked straight ahead as he drove
off, one hand raised in greeting to us.

SASQUATCH SIGHTINGS

Sasquatch says the budgie was never well in itself since Matt Dillon shot it.

The only person who believes this is Harpo, a respected fabulist in his own right. He explained that the Matt Dillon involved was one James Arness, completely irresponsible with a handgun. His sidekick was Dennis Weaver, and he didn't have a limp either, not in Gunlaw anyway. And he followed up with one of his own specials, about how in English law, and in the time of capital punishment, any person they failed to hang properly three times got an automatic pardon. And Harpo knew personally the last man to be so reprieved. Somehow the mechanism jammed each time the lever was pulled; the executioner had been completely baffled. The reprieved man, Harpo says, was a well-known figure perambulating in the purlieus of Failsworth; mind you, he says, he had an extremely long neck, like a giraffe.

This is generally considered a myth of note in Ravensgill, but my guess is it's the stark truth. Sasquatch didn't see the connection with his budgie dropping off her perch when Matt Dillon fired his revolver on TV. 'I just thought you'd enjoy a bit of a laugh,' said Harpo. Sasquatch knocked him to the ground; he apologized at length and every day for three weeks, but a pet was a pet to him; the budgie had finally died after nine years of nervous dyspepsia, and it didn't do to come between a man and his grief. Harpo thought himself lucky to be walking, and suffered the apologies humbly and with suppressed yawns. Sasquatch paid to have Harpo's dentures mended.

You don't call him Sasquatch, not to his face: Nelson Wragg, demolition, thirty years, mill buildings, chimneys, people. In his pomp, he could shin up a chimney without laddering it, drop a rope for hammer and pick, and fell it brick by brick from under his feet. A troll that wanted to be Lucifer, dreaming of lost empires he never had (the most he got was ninety days for looting), setting his foot on the neck of the heathen, whose civilization and culture went back ten thousand years before Sasquatch learned to tie his bootlaces Indian Army style, he weeps with pride on Armistice Day.

He has a square-rigged schooner tattoo'd on his vast chest among the grizzled wool. When he was still living with his wife, and had been in town, you'd see him weaving his way up from the bus, grazing the walls at both sides, preceded by a gaggle of lads full of snorts and whispered explosions ('Looker him, looker him, looker his *trousers. .*'), his shirt open to the waist. Ada would be on the doorstep, waiting. . .

'He's coming Mrs Wragg!'
'Where is he!? Where is he, the drunken whiskery fat-lipped stinking *get*!?'
'He's just coming up Pin Lane Mrs Wragg!'
'Where is he?! I'll scuttle his ship for him!'
And she did, four-square on the schooner. She never missed, and Sasquatch never seemed to have any recollection of what spreadeagled him: the broom-handle, rambang amidships. And even in his fifties it took six coppers to down him. I think his skull must be thicker than most people's, it certainly *looks* thicker, with brows like buttresses. A young man, wishing to prove a point, broke a bottle of brown ale over his head. There was a silence when even the jukebox seemed to have a thick blanket over it. The

brown ale and blood slowly filled Nelson's eyebrows. . .
'If that's your best,' said Nelson, 'then you *are*
in trouble.'

Then he was mugged. Down by the allotments, of all
places. He says they jumped him from behind, he doesn't
know how many, but it felt like a rugby scrum armed with
hammers. When the law had finished with them, they'd
have him to deal with, he said, he'd break their ribs for
'em. But his rage was not the rage of a citizen unlawfully
set upon and deprived of his wallet, not to me. We've had
young out-of-works recently, from the towns, bag-snatch-
ing, burgling (the village burglars can be counted on two
fingers, and are, every time there's a break-in), but this
was a fall as big as any chimney he'd dropped. The dust
and rubble of a felled titan. 'All I've got is my strength,' he
told me, 'if I'm poorly, I hardly exist. A bunch a muscles.'
His eyes filled with tears. I moved further down the bar.
It's a bad sign when he starts crying, he gets to roaring
soon after, like a bull in a pen, and his fists get bigger.

To get out from under the rambling apologies over the
budgie incident, Harpo suggested another pet. What
about a bull terrier of impeccable pedigree? He carefully
avoided saying that a dog might afford some protection
against footpads, but Sasquatch became very quiet and
attentive at once. Dog's Doogle Eye had a Staffordshire
Bull Terrier much given to phantom pregnancies; Lillian
Bentham had a spectacular randy dog of the same breed. I
say randy because it rips panels out of front doors to get at
a bitch on heat. Prior to the time I'm talking about, it had
never been to a bitch. It knows all about it now, and rips
doors. A delegation was made up to wait on Lillian; you
need two or three of you to talk to Lillian because on your
own she can bring you to desperation over a simple
exchange like 'Good morning'.

'D.H. hasn't been a daddy yet,' she said,

peeking round the door, blinking in the daylight.

'What a perfectly lovely name, D.H.,' said Harpo.

'He's named after the famous writer,' she said.

'What famous writer?' said Dog's Doogle Eye.

'It was Alex's idea,' she said.

'Lawrence,' said Harpo.

'No, Alex is his name,' she said. 'I should know Desmond, he is my husband after all. Lawrence is the writer, D. H. Lawrence. We called the dog after him.'

Her eyes darted from face to face, she seemed to be panicking already; Sasquatch tried for light chat, a Mountain Gorilla peeling a hard-boiled egg.

'Been easier if you'd called him Lawrence, wouldn't it? then you wouldn't have to explain every time.'

'Not if his name's Alex,' she said, a pale trembling hand to her lips.

'Dog's Doogle Eye's got a bull terrier bitch, and it's coming into season just,' said Harpo, hasty, 'wouldn't you like one of your D.H.'s offspring to be his little friend?'

'Are you sure he won't be worried, and let himself down?'

A swift, ice-cold glimpse here, into Lillian and Alex Bentham's marital life.

'I shall be officiating personally Lillian,' said Harpo, 'and I happen to know Stuart's bitch is of the most docile disposition.'

'It killed an Airedale this morning,' said Dog's Doogle Eye, mildly defensive.

They persuaded Lillian to open the door again; the union was arranged, bride's owner to pay all expenses; Lillian to be witness. Doogle started to shake over the expenses bit, until Harpo got him on one side and asked him to concentrate extremely hard, and try to imagine what scintilla of expenses there could remotely be. The place, the canal towpath, where parties could observe (over the wall) without being publicly branded for prurience. Calendars were consulted, *The Sherley Book of Dogs* borrowed.

As things turned out later, they needn't have bothered putting the bitch in Doogle Eye's van to smuggle her past the Ravensgill canine rantipoles. Harpo crouched down in the passenger seat, gripping the dog's collar to hold it in the back: the saga had leaked out, irresistibly, and they didn't want a crowd at the wedding. P.C. Harry Mooney, looking down from the driver's seat of the police Land-rover on this interesting sight, pulled out to overtake and investigate. Dog's Doogle Eye accelerated. Harry pressed his foot down and started the blue flashing light. Dog did a screw turn onto the Ashton road, the exhaust pipe, lacy with corrosion, thundering beneath their bums and filling the van with fumes. 'What in Heaven's name's coming to pass Stuart?' said Harpo, hurled against the frail clattering door as they swooped again, under the railway viaduct.

'Cop car,' said Dog's Doogle Eye.

The bitch was presumably used to the acrid smell, the ear-damaging clangour, and to being thrown about among the first-aid boxes and bargain samples in the back; it stood at the rear windows, watching the police car lurch after them, scrambling up again eagerly after every swivel and swing of the van. Harpo stuck his head out and looked back; 'That's Harry Mooney,' he waved a Duke of Edinburgh greeting. An Ashton Police Capri was slewed across the road, and two large P.C.s stood waiting for them, solemn and solid. Harpo barked 'STOP', and Dog anchored up by reflex. When he realized what he'd done, he clenched his knuckles white over the steering wheel in a sudden spasm of despair. 'I can't *stand* back seat drivers,' he said.

Harry's face, made immense by the helmet, loomed at the window. The two Ashton P.C.s behind, a dark force, blocking the light, watchful of Harpo. 'Is it a stolen vehicle?' asked one of them. Harry realized he'd not much chance of Doogle Eye knowing the number of his van: he never owned one long enough to learn the number; he also realized he was going to look somewhat of a nana in front of his colleagues if he didn't take charge. He pulled open the driver's side door, leaned down, elbow on the door, the other hand gripping the roof.

'Explain,' he said.

Harpo eased out his side, a polite nod to the alerted P.C.s. He sidled casually forward. Harry still leaned down, head bowed, as if praying that Dog's Doogle Eye would come up with something rational. Harpo pee'd, debonair and worldly, against the wheel. Five pairs of eyes raised to heaven, five minds with but a single thought: 'Nearside front wheel.' He zipped up, moved to Harry's side, discreet.

> 'An interesting piece of folklore about pissing on wheels in the carriageway,' said Harry, 'but it applies only to horse-drawn vehicles.'
> 'How vastly intriguing,' said Harpo, 'no doubt a mode of ensuring that a draught horse is not left unattended in a public thoroughfare.' He lowered his voice, the courier brings a matter of state to the Minister, 'We were just taking his bitch to be mated. Sasquatch will be waiting. Canal towpath.'

The canal was two miles back, towards Ravensgill. Harry's mouth stretched in a taut parody of a smile over the aloe bitterness of a village copper's life.

'Don't do it to me, Desmond,' he said; 'you were crouched down.'

'Didn't want to draw attention to myself,' murmured Harpo, his gaze on the middle distance.

Luckily the two Ashton coppers, fascinated as they were by the desultory mumbles at the van, were occupied directing traffic round the scattered vehicles, so Harry didn't have any damnfool explanations to invent for them.

'Right, bring them along to the Police Station within twenty-four hours,' he told Doogle Eye, loud for his colleagues' ears, and swung back to his Landrover, making like Officer in Charge.

'It's a good job he didn't ask me for my driving licence, tax and insurance, MOT and log book,' said Dog.

'He just did.'

'Did he? I haven't got them with me.'

'Stuart, you haven't got them anywhere.'

'Criticize criticize, that's all you know.'

Lillian hadn't arrived when they found Sasquatch by the canal. He stood, square and still as an ox in a field, unaware of late or early. Dog's Doogle Eye was still stiff with indignation that even his own friend should pick on him, let alone the police. Harpo persuaded him that Lillian would be more cooperative if he put his teeth in. Then she arrived, towed by D.H. like a tin can on a wedding car. Doogle Eye was holding his bitch on the field side of the wall, but D.H. found her. Sasquatch grabbed Lillian and released the groom just in time to stop him from dragging her over the wall and into the nuptials. Doogle Eye leapt back onto the canal towpath with a high scream of terror as D.H. came the other way, a quivering pack of bunched and purposeful muscle, fangs agape.

Lillian was overdressed for the canal side; fine for a Ducal reception, except perhaps the high red boots; the candy-pink dress coat was a treat; so anyway, quite a lot had to be straightened when Nelson put her down. When she came round from her flurry of finery, she explained that she didn't want the neighbours to know exactly where she was going, and had anyone such a thing as a tissue?

Three male backs, hunched and silent to regard the primal scene on the other side of the wall. Harpo offered a few words on his astounding success with animals.

'I was having a light supper of lamb chop, chips and petits pois, on the coffee table as I watched TV,' he said, 'and was keeping the lamb chop till last, in order to savour it longer. I gradually became aware of the cat's paw, groping round delicately from underneath the table. An extraordinarily intelligent animule, which I attribute to my early cultivation of its intellect: when it was a kitten, and Maggie and me were on non-speakers, I used to read bits out of the newspaper to it. It drove Margaret absolutely insane. I was mesmerized by this slowly palpating small paw, dabbing about until it found the chop, and swiftly gripped it with the claws, whipping it under the table. I sprang to my feet with a yell of outrage. The cat hastened upstairs, hoppity hoppity, on three legs and a lamb chop. I got the chop back, but it had all fluff on it.'

Lillian waited a moment to see if she could grasp the point of this story, or whether one of the three might acknowledge her presence.

'I hope D.H. will be gentle,' she said.

'I shan't forget you for this job, Des,' said Sasquatch, 'I know how to be grateful.'

'What about me? and Lillian?' said Dog's
Doogle Eye.
'I reckon I'll have a bitch, eh?' said Sasquatch,
'more faithful.'
'Indubitably,' said Harpo.
'A dog'll never let you down, where people will.'
'I haven't let you down Nelson,' said Doogle
Eye.
'Are you sure you should be watching?' said
Lillian, 'might it not upset the. . couple?'
'This pup'll never leave my side till it's fully
trained,' said Sasquatch. 'What I used to do
with the budgie was to blow up its beak.'
'Did it do any good?' asked Harpo.
'Not really. It fell off its perch you know.'
'It's called bonding that.'
'Falling off a perch?'
'Blowing up a animule's nose. Wouldn't really
do for budgies, they're not pack animules; they
don't bond.'
'Flock,' said Sasquatch.
'Pardon?' said Lillian.
'You can bite their scruff too, make them
faithful. I don't think I'll ever get over the
shock of realizing Ada wasn't steadfast to me,'
said Sasquatch.
'Women are like that,' said Dog's Doogle Eye,
'just don't understand when you're short, and
they have to manage. She says she'll go out to
work herself, and I'll have to manage.'
Sasquatch moved his head slowly to examine Dog's
Doogle Eye, turned away again.
'Whenever I look at you, Stuart,' he said, 'I
realize I'm an intelligent, stable, normal human
being.'

A silence fell, only the ripple of the river on the other side of the field, an occasional car on the road beyond, and Doogle Eye's stertorous resentment. Lillian was getting lonely. Were they all right? The silence, the three backs. If it's not rude to watch, it's certainly rude not to answer a person's civil question. Lillian's febrile need to have attention paid to her anxieties usually shows in small hysterical retreats; this time she shoved Dog's Doogle Eye brusquely to one side, and looked. And looked. She gripped Sasquatch's huge forefinger convulsively.

'I may pass out,' she said.

The dogs stood, rear to rear, linked by pink, their eyes rolled up to the audience, mournful as a Christmas card; the union was complete.

> 'Dog-locked,' said Harpo. 'You see Lillian, the female canine has numerous wombs to be fertilized. .' (a hazy recollection here of an illustration from the *Book of Dogs*). . 'it's a phenomenon of the biological interaction of pooches that they take a long time at it. Brings tears to your eyes doesn't it? Stuart, please don't.'

Dog's Doogle Eye was sharpening his Swiss Army (type) knife on the Millstone Grit of the wall, a noise near the threshold of pain.

> 'I don't have to put up with this, Harpo,' said Doogle Eye, 'you all pick on me.'
> 'What's he going to do?' said Lillian.
> 'Nothing,' said Harpo, 'he's going to keep silent, he's going to stop trembling and making that cacchinatous noise.'

Doogle Eye's resentments surged up.

> 'You use these words, Desmond, I don't think you even know yourself what they mean, but my resentments surge up.'

'It means a noise like raucous laughter,' said
Harpo.
'I want to know what he intends to do with that
knife,' said Lillian. 'D.H. is stuck.'
'They'll have to be separated eventually,' said
Sasquatch.

It says a lot for Lillian's emotional sturdiness that she
didn't pass out right then, but her habit of fraying other
people's nerve-ends to her own chronic pain level stood
steady.

'I'm not having you cut his thingy,' she said,
breathless, 'he's only just found out.'
'Let Stuart have his fun Mrs Bentham,'
Sasquatch enjoys a crisis; he turned back to
watch the glum unmoving couple; 'that dog'll be
a happy animal after, no further worries.'

The whole thing escalated, Harpo says it escalated, and I
believe him, as I believe everything he says: a soaring
unsteady pyramid of misapprehension.

'I shall attack you,' said Lillian, to Dog, biting
her lip like a berserk, eyes starting.
'Whaffor?' said Doogle Eye, still busy with his
knife.

Sasquatch's face was daemonic, his fleshy moist lips close
to her ear:

'You could blow on it a bit Mrs Bentham, that
might do it; don't take it out on Stuart just
when he's trying to help. He was only thinking
of a nick.'

She'd scrambled over the wall before anyone fully knew
what was agate, staggered slightly on her high heels in the
soft pasture, and bent to blow, watched by two dogs that
didn't know it was going to be like this, three men who
didn't believe it, and the rush-hour double-decker bus,
cruising by on the Ashton road, every window a face. A

pink-coated dainty figure, holding back her hair to defuse Nature's time-bomb.

Did I say the whole exercise, if epic, was futile? Well, Nelson visited the nursing bitch daily from the time she came to term, inspected the litter of identical bald-bellied squirming whelps, sagely selecting the finest specimen. Dog's Doogle Eye said he'd priced pedigree Staffordshires, and put in an order for a new van. The notion of paying cash, and for a brand new vehicle, made him dizzy. He said he was fed up of looking for smooth places on the footpath so't he didn't wear out his shoes, and they had some superb trousers on the Market, seconds, but you couldn't tell, so how hard you looked. Sasquatch said if he didn't stop nitter-nattering in his earole about money, Doogle Eye would soon be walking about with his head the other way round. Harpo explained that Lillian was entitled to pick of the litter, free. Doogle Eye said Lillian didn't want pick of the litter, in fact she wouldn't open the door to him even, and that husband of hers wasn't civil either, Lawrence or whatever he was called. In that case, said Harpo, there'd be a stud fee for her. A stud fee? what had *she* done? What had Stuart done, Harpo enquired. Dog's Doogle Eye got agitated and incoherent after that, though the bit about his rent arrears was clear enough. He went missing for three crucial weeks, Sasquatch in agony for his new pup's welfare. He kept shoving cod-liver oil capsules through the letterbox at Doogle Eye's flat, but was the pup getting them? Then they found him, in an Oldham public house known only to seven other people. I never heard even the gist of the conversation, but they settled for a fiver towards the expenses of rearing, and Nelson bore his love-bucket home, for training in attack and defence. Then Dog's Doogle Eye went missing again: he'd sold the remaining pups for prices from twenty to fifty pounds, according to the number of letters the

Arrears Office had sent him, and the customers, less tyrannical than Sasquatch to start with, began to seek him out.

The pup grew, tall and rangy for a bull terrier, black and white, with one ear flopped and one pricked. You could hear Sasquatch training it in his allotment shed, 'SIT!', he would bellow, 'WALKIES!!' He'd lead it forth in the village on a stout cord, tugging at it to show admirers and enquirers its brute power and attacking instincts, 'FRIEND!', his eyes red with emotion.

> 'It'll let anyone into the shed,' he said, 'but you try getting out again. It even had me.'

Sure enough, there was a red weal on his nose.

> 'I'll break your back you little swine,' he said fondly; 'I was blowing up its nose to make it bond itself to me.'

It seemed an equable enough animal, silent and obedient when in the street, though he assured me it still attacked him if he surprised it in any way. His own fault, he said, for bringing out its inbred savagery, and did anti-tetanus last a good while? By eight months, it was twenty-two inches at the shoulder, and had a long, fine, whippet nose.

I suppose we all came to the same conclusion, within days of each other, but no one cared to discuss it with the owner. Sasquatch has a sense of humour, but Dog's Doogle Eye didn't come round to test it. Harpo passed the allotments. The pup was chewing at Sasquatch's Perpetual Spinach.

> 'What a magnificent animule that pup has turned out to be, Nelson,' he remarked, 'a credit to you and to its. .'

He was going to say 'breeding', but it flashed into his mind with a chill clarity whose idea had generated the whole fiasco. Sasquatch's eyes were pools of thick tears. The words 'pup', 'dog', 'Staffordshire', 'pedigree', 'breeding', banged about in Harpo's mind like seamines on a rip tide.

  'Stuart was telling me about a completely bald man,' he gabbled, 'no beard, nothing under his arms, not even eyelashes. I couldn't think what the right word was, I said was he an albino? No, no, says Stuart, as a matter of fact he came from Accrington.'

  'Why are you telling me this?' said Sasquatch.

  'I'm having trouble with certain words.'

  'What words?'

  'I don't want to say.'

  'What words?' Sasquatch's fists were getting enormous.

  'Well, I didn't want to say "Dog's Doogle Eye", but I found myself mentioning him, I thought you might be annoyed with him.'

  'I am annoyed with him. What words?'

  'Erm, "breeding"; I thought I'd better keep off mentioning that.'

Sasquatch knocked him through the Gartside's greenhouse. He took him to Casualty to have his stitches. He'd take him to have them out, but Harpo's avoiding him just now, the apologies depress him.

  D.H., it seems, was not the first.

THE GHOST OF THE MAD MONK (III)

Oh yes, I was going to tell you about the time Bakey hid hisself when we were mucking about in the old Dyeworks wasn't I? I was saying how we pinched some dye powder, and dyed the little dam green. And Bakey bolting the door behind me in the upstairs part, and getting me going about the Ghost of the Mad Monk, and rats, and then making phooooom phooooom noises by blowing across the neck of the big jar. He must think I'm the biggest tater in the world. Mind, it was a good laugh when old Clarky was lecturing us about algae making the little dam green. We made up a song about it.

> The finest sight you've ever seen
> When Algernon made the dam pea-green
> Old Clarky yelled just look at this
> Something here has gone amiss
> The water once was clear and clean
> Now Algy's pittle has made it green
> Get him into hospital get him into bed
> Get a tater pie and stick it on his head
> Pee po bum belly district nurse draws
> Old Algernon's as sick as a horse.

When I realized Bakey was having me on, making the phoom noises, I thought I'll give him phoom, I'll creep down while he's busy, and give him a touch of the Mad Monks; I'll get right up behind him, and I'll murmur in his earole, I am the Ghost of the Mad Monk, I'll say, and this is my Revenge.

I got to the bottom of the steps, and peered round to where the jars were. No flummin' sign of him of course. I walked along the cobbles, keeping close to the wall, on the watchout for Bakey. Good practice for the Resistance. All was silent. I went up the stairs to the door of the room where we'd first been. The door was open, just a crack. I held my breath, and squeezed in, making sure the door didn't move, and squeak, and betray my presence. Inside, I kept very still, by the door, and moved my eyes round, to see if he was hidden anywhere. A heap of mucky rags in one corner, in the shadows. The far door still bolted, I could see where the rust had scraped off a bit. Then I looked again at the heap of rags. Bakey's shoe, and his sock, just showing. What a dope he must think I am. I eased out of the door. Pulled it closed behind me, and slid the bolt in. That'll teach him. He can have his rats now, and his Mad Monk. And I went home.

After tea, I strolled back. I reckoned he'd be about raving barmy by now. I was whistling as I went up the stairs. Unbolted the door. I bring a Free Pardon from His Majesty, I shouted, Bakey, thou art a prisoner no longer. Silence. What a dope: the other door was bolted from the inside. He'd be home by now, laughing and snorting over me. The far door was still bolted. I couldn't figure it out. If he'd gone out that way, how could it still be bolted? I went and unbolted it. Pushed at the door. There was something stopping it. It was as if Bakey spoke to me, though the whole place was silent, except for my breathing: 'The work of the Ghost of the Mad Monk.' I dived on the pile of rags and threw them about. He wasn't there. How long do rats take to eat a human being? I listened; no scratching and squeaking. Supposing he'd been lying there, struck down by a mysterious disease, when I'd seen his shoe and sock sticking out? He wouldn't cover himself over if he was struck down with a mysterious disease. Would he?

On the way home, there was this policeman. Good evening constable, I said, I bet you walk round the old Dyeworks pretty regular eh? Keep moving son, he said, or you'll feel the weight of my hand. I was beginning to get sweaty and cold. I called at Bakey's house. Is Ronald coming out, I said, smiling as best I could to make it seem ordinary. He's not in, said his mum, I'll tell him you called; where will you be? I thought Australia, but I didn't say it. I don't know I said. I kept my teeth uncovered, to make it seem like a smile still, it was pretty dark by now. All right, she said. They never know where Bakey is. As I passed the kitchen window, she was saying to Bakey's dad Got teeth like piano keys that lad hasn't he? would you say he was a bit simple?

I don't know how or when I got to sleep that night, but I had some rotten dreams; Bakey, the Ghost of the Mad Monk, gasping and groaning, me in hospital with a mysterious disease.

Next morning at Assembly, no Bakey. English first. No Bakey. He'd vanished. And it was my fault. I couldn't concentrate on anything, it was like a grey dream, people moving about, old Clarky shouting, kids muttering and passing messages under desks. No Bakey.

Suddenly, there he was, at the classroom door, I could see his stupid head, hair nearly cropped bald, through the frosted glass. He came in. 'WHAT TIME D'YOU CALL THIS BATESON?' said Clarky. 'Had a nosebleed sir.' Clarky didn't believe a word of it. 'GET TO YOUR PLACE, FUTILE BOY,' he said. I could see crusty blood round Bakey's nostrils. Brilliant he is, nosebleed, any time. My dad found the envelope of green dye-powder, he muttered to me, he was shaving, and it fell off the top of the cabinet where I'd hidden it. He's got a green chin now. I knew he'd bash me, so I had a nosebleed before he'd stopped roaring. Where the flummin' heck were you? I said. When? he muttered. After I locked you in. You didn't lock me in. I flummin' did. You locked my sock and shoe in, not me, he says. I thought, come break-time, he'll have another nosebleed, from me. The other door was blocked, I said, it had something against it, I couldn't open it. Be the Mad Monk, that, he said.

He must be the biggest flummin' liar in the whole universe, Bakey.

SHELTERED HOUSING

ENID COURT
PRESTON
MINSTER
LAMBOURNE

Thanet 16/12/86